"Anthony Horowitz is the lion of children's literature." Michael Morpurgo

"Horowitz has become a writer who converts boys to reading."
The Times

"A first-class children's novelist."
TES

THE DIAMOND BROTHERS IN...

Four of Diamonds

THE DIAMOND BROTHERS IN...

Four of Diamonds

ANTHONY HOROWITZ

WALKER
BOOKS

First published individually as *The French Confection* (2002),
The Blurred Man (2002), *I Know What You Did Last Wednesday* (2002)
and *The Greek Who Stole Christmas* (2007) by Walker Books Ltd
87 Vauxhall Walk, London SE11 5HJ

This edition published 2012

2 4 6 8 10 9 7 5 3 1

*The French Confection, The Blurred Man, I Know What You
Did Last Wednesday* © 2002 Gameslayer Ltd
The Greek Who Stole Christmas © 2007
Stormbreaker Productions Ltd
Introduction © 2007 Gameslayer Ltd
Cover illustrations © 2012 Tony Ross

The right of Anthony Horowitz to be identified as author of this work
has been asserted by him in accordance with the
Copyright, Designs and Patents Act 1988

This book has been typeset in Sabon

Printed in Great Britain by Clays Ltd, St Ives plc

British Library Cataloguing in Publication Data:
a catalogue record for this book is available from the British Library

ISBN 978-1-4063-4145-4

www.walker.co.uk

CONTENTS

I Know What You Did Last Wednesday

The Greek Who Stole Christmas

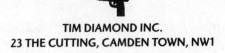

Dear Reader,

It's been a while since I had lunch with the chairman of Walker Books. He's an old man now. Most of his hair's gone white and the rest of it's just gone. He wears bi-focal glasses but he doesn't really need them. He's forgotten how to read. He'd forget his own name if it wasn't written on his Zimmer frame.

And yet I still remember the day he took me out – just the two of us, face to face, though with a face like his I wouldn't have bothered. We met at the poshest restaurant in London ... then crossed the road to the café on the other side. He ordered two bacon sandwiches without the bacon. He was a vegetarian. And that was when he tried to sweet-talk me into writing an introduction for this collection of stories. But it takes more than a bag of sweets to get Tim Diamond on your side, so I told Walker to take a walk.

A few days later he came tiptoeing round my flat with a bag of books: a bit like Santa Claus without the beard, the laughter or (it was the middle of June) Christmas. This was his deal. Three dozen adventures of Maisy mouse and an old Where's Wally? annual in return for a couple of pages by me. But as far as I was concerned, there was still one book missing. The Walker cheque book ... preferably autographed. Unfortunately, when I pointed this out, the chairman just scowled. That was the sort of man he was: small, hard-edged and leathery. Just like his chair.

"I need an introduction!" he cried.

"All right. How do you do, I'm Tim Diamond," I said.

"No, no, no. For the book!"

"Why do you need an introduction?" Nick – my kid brother – asked. "You probably won't sell any copies anyway."

Actually, in the end, it was Nick who talked me into writing this. He reminded me it's only thanks to Walker that I've become known as England's sharpest, most successful private eye, the sort of detective that makes Hercule Poirot look like a short Belgian with a funny moustache! I have to admit that Walker have been behind me all the way. About thirty miles behind me.

They launched this book with a slap-up dinner at the Ritz. The service was so slow, the waiters deserved to be slapped. Twelve journalists came, but only eleven left. That was how bad the food was.

At the same time, they took out a full-page ad in British Airways "High Life" magazine. They were hoping the books would fly off the shelves and the funny thing is, they did. Maybe it was the new covers that had been specially designed to stop people noticing the new price. It certainly couldn't have been the title. The last time I got the four of diamonds in a high class poker game, I went home without my clothes. If they are going to name a book after a playing card, they could have at least chosen a king.

Anyway, here's the introduction. I'm not quite sure how to begin. Introducing the introduction is always the hardest part. I'm glad I'm not a writer. And if you met the guy who does the writing for me, you'd be glad too.

His name is Anthony Horowitz – and I use him to put my adventures down on paper. Let me tell you a bit about him. A lot of people have compared him to JK Rowling. They say he's not as good. He has a wife, two sons, a stuffed dog and a word processor, and the word processor is the only one that doesn't want to leave home. You ever see "Foyle's War", "Midsomer Murders" or "Collision" on TV? Me neither – but he wrote them all. They're the only programmes people fast-forward through to see the advertisements. He also writes a lot of books. About thirty of them at the last count. Enough books to immobilise a mobile library.

I met him just after I'd cracked the case that became known as "The Falcon's Malteser". I don't think his career was doing too well just then. How many other writers tap-dance outside Harrods in their spare time? Anyway, I told him my story, he began to write – and the rest was history. Actually, nobody wanted history. They wanted an adventure. So he had to write it a second time. But it worked. "The Falcon's Malteser" sold twenty-seven copies in Waterstone's the day it was published and I only bought twenty-six of them. Soon we were right at number one in the Bookseller chart. OK – it was the remainders chart but you've got to start somewhere. "The Times" critic said the book was "hysterical" and she should know.

Since then, I've cracked more cases than the entire baggage-handling department at Heathrow Airport, and Horowitz has written them all. "Public Enemy Number Two", "South by South East" – one day maybe he'll come up with a title that somebody actually understands. I had a pretty hairy time in Australia recently and he says that'll come out in a book too. Apparently the title is going to be: "The Radius of the Lost Shark".

Which brings me to the book you are now holding in your hand (unless you didn't buy it, in which case it's still on the shelf ... a bit like my editor). The four stories in this book all happened to me in the space of one year and all I can say is, I'm glad it wasn't a leap year. One extra day would have been the death of me.

Why do so many people want to kill me? I could have been plastered all over Paris in "The French Confection". I was nearly shot in "The Blurred Man" and the next time I go on the Millennium Wheel, I want to be sure I'm going to make it the whole way round. There were so many murders in "I Know What You Did Last Wednesday" that it's a miracle I wasn't one of them. And as for "The Greek Who Stole Christmas" ... well, next year I'm giving that particular holiday season a miss. Tinsel, turkeys and gift-wrapped hand grenades? No thanks.

You may have noticed that this edition is printed on special cheap paper and as for the glue ... all I can say is, don't leave it out in the sun. The book is also carbon neutral. A forest in Norway was cut down to produce it but the good news is that another one was planted ... in England. The Norwegians have got too many anyway. You might like to know, ten per cent of every copy sold goes to a very worthwhile charity. Me. I have an overdraft and a hungry kid brother to support.

One last thing. Remember that this book comes with a MONEY BACK GUARANTEE. If for any reason you don't like it, Walker guarantee they won't give you back your money.

All the best,

Tim Diamond

THE FRENCH CONFECTION

THE FRENCH
FOR MURDER

Everybody loves Paris. There's an old guy who even wrote a song about it. "I love Paris in the springtime...", that's how it goes. Well, all I can say is, he obviously never went there with my big brother, Tim. I did – and it almost killed me.

It all started with a strawberry yoghurt.

It was a French strawberry yoghurt, of course, and it was all we had in the fridge for breakfast. Tim and I tossed a coin to decide who'd get the first mouthful. Then we tossed the coin to see who'd keep the coin. Tim won both times. So there I was sitting at the breakfast table chewing my nails, which was all I had to chew, when Tim suddenly let out a great gurgle and started waving his spoon in the air like he was trying to swat a fly.

"What is it, Tim?" I asked. "Don't tell me! You've found a strawberry!"

"No, Nick! Look…!"

He was holding up the silver foil that he'd just torn off the yoghurt carton and looking at it, and now I understood. The company that made the yoghurt was having one of those promotions. You've probably seen them on chocolate bars or crisps or Coke cans. These days you can't even open a can of beans without finding out if you've won a car or a holiday in Mexico or a cheque for a thousand pounds. Personally, I'm just grateful if I actually find some beans. Anyway, the yoghurt people were offering a whole range of prizes and there it was, written on the underside of the foil.

Congratulations from Bestlé Fruit Yoghurts! You have just won a weekend for two in Paris! Just telephone the number printed on the carton for further details and … Bon Voyage!

"I've won, Nick!" Tim gasped. "A weekend for two…!" He stopped and bit his thumb. "Who shall I take?" he muttered.

"Oh thanks a lot, Tim," I said. "It was me who bought the yoghurt."

"But it was my money."

"If it hadn't been for me, you'd have spent it on a choc-ice."

Tim scowled. "But Paris, Nick! It's the most romantic city in Europe. I want to take my girlfriend."

16

"Tim," I reminded him. "You haven't got a girlfriend."

That was a bit cruel of me. The truth was, Tim hadn't been very lucky in love. His first serious relationship had ended tragically when his girlfriend had tried to murder him. After that he'd replied to one of those advertisements in the lonely hearts column of a newspaper, but he can't have read it properly because the girl had turned out to be a guy who spent the evening chasing him round Paddington station. His last girlfriend had been a fire eater in a local circus. He'd taken her out for a romantic, candlelit dinner but she'd completely spoiled it by eating the candles. Right now he was on his own. He sometimes said he felt like a monk – but without the haircut or the religion.

Anyway, we argued a bit more but finally he picked up the telephone and rang the number on the yoghurt carton. There was no answer.

"That's because you've telephoned the sell-by date," I told him. I turned the carton over. "This is the number here…"

And that was how, three weeks later, we found ourselves standing in the forecourt at Waterloo station. Tim was carrying the tickets. I was carrying the bags. It had been more than a year since we'd been abroad – that had been to Amsterdam on the trail of the mysterious assassin known as Charon – and that time we

17

had gone by ferry. Tim had been completely seasick even before he reached the sea. I was relieved that this time we were going by train, taking the Channel Tunnel, although with Tim, of course, you never knew.

We took the escalator down to the international terminal. Ahead of us, the tunnel was waiting: a thirty-two mile stretch linking England and France, built at a cost of twelve billion pounds.

"You have to admit," Tim said. "It's an engineering marvel."

"That's just what I was thinking," I said.

"Yes. It's a fantastic escalator. And so much faster than going down the stairs…"

We had two seats next to each other right in the middle of one of the carriages. The train was pretty full and soon we were joined by two other passengers opposite us. They were both travelling alone. The first was from Texas – you could tell just from his hat. He was chewing an unlit cigar (this was a non-smoking compartment) and reading a magazine: *International Oil*. The other passenger was a very old lady with white hair and skin so wrinkled I was amazed it managed to stay on. I wasn't sure if she had huge eyes or extremely powerful spectacles but every time she looked at me I thought I was about to be hit by a pair of grey and white golf balls. I looked out of the window. The platform was already empty, sweeping in a graceful curve beneath the great glass canopy. Somewhere a door slammed.

The train left exactly on time at ten minutes past ten. There was no whistle. No announcement. I wouldn't have known we had moved if it hadn't been for the slight shudder – and even that was Tim, not the train. He was obviously excited.

About an hour later there was an announcement on the intercom and we dipped into the tunnel carved out underneath the sea. That was a non-event too. A car-park, a sign advertising hamburgers, a white cement wall and suddenly the outside world disappeared to be replaced by rushing blackness. So this was the engineering miracle of the last century? As far as Eurostar was concerned, it was just a hole in the ground.

Tim had been ready with his camera and now he drew back, disappointed. "Is this it?" he demanded.

I looked up from my book. "What were you expecting, Tim?" I asked.

"I thought this train went under water!" Tim sighed. "I wanted to take some pictures of the fish!"

The other passengers had heard this and somehow it broke the silence. The old lady had been knitting what looked like a multi-coloured sack but now she looked up. "I love taking the train," she announced, and for the first time I realized that she was French. Her accent was so thick you could have wrapped yourself in it to keep warm.

"It sure is one hell of a thing," the Texan agreed. "London to Paris in three and a half hours. Great for business."

The Texan held up his magazine. "I'm in oil. Jed Mathis is the name."

"Why do you call your oil Jed Mathis?" Tim asked.

"I'm sorry?" Jed looked confused. He turned to the old lady. "Are you visiting your grandchildren in Paris?" he asked.

"Non!" the lady replied.

Tim dug into his pocket and pulled out a French dictionary. While he was looking up the word, she continued in English.

"I have a little cake shop in Paris. Erica Nice. That's my name. Please, you must try some of my almond slices." And before anyone could stop her, she'd pulled out a bag of cakes which she offered to us all.

We were still hurtling through the darkness. Tim put away his dictionary and helped himself. At the same time, a steward approached us, pushing one of those trolleys piled up with sandwiches and coffee. He was a thin, pale man with a drooping moustache and slightly sunken eyes. The name on his badge was Marc Chabrol. I remember thinking even then that he looked nervous. A nervous traveller, I thought.

20

But then, why would a nervous traveller work on a train?

Jed produced a wallet full of dollars and offered to buy us all coffee. A free breakfast and we hadn't even arrived. Things were definitely looking up.

"So what do you do?" Erica Nice asked, turning to Tim.

Tim gave a crooked smile. It was meant to make him look smart but in fact he just looked as though he had toothache. "I'm a private detective," he said.

The steward dropped one of the coffee cups. Fortunately, he hadn't added the water yet. Coffee granules showered over the KitKats.

"A private detective?" Erica trilled. "How very unusual!"

"Are you going to Paris on business?" the Texan asked.

Now of course the answer was "no". We were on holiday. Tim hadn't had any business for several weeks and even then he had only been hired to find a missing dog. In fact he had spent three days at Battersea Dogs' Home where he had been bitten three times – twice by dogs. The trouble was, though, he was never going to admit this. He liked to think of himself as a man of mystery. So now he winked and leaned forward. "Just between you and me," he drawled, "I'm on a case." Yes. A nutcase, I thought. But he went on.

"I've been hired by Interplop."

"You mean Interpol," the Texan said.

"The International Police," Tim agreed. "It's a top-secret case. It's so secret, they don't even know about it at the top. In other words..." He gestured with his almond slice, spraying Jed with crumbs, "...a case for Tim Diamond."

The steward had obviously heard all this. As he put down the first cup of coffee, his hands were shaking so much that the liquid spilled over the table. His face had been pale to begin with. Now it had no colour at all. Even his moustache seemed to have faded.

"Where are you staying in Paris?" the old lady asked.

"It's a hotel called The Fat Greek," Tim said.

"Le Chat Gris," I corrected him. It was French for "grey cat" and this was the name of the hotel where Bestlé Yoghurts had booked us in for three nights.

The name seemed to have an electric effect on the steward. I'd been watching him out of the corner of my eye and actually saw him step backwards, colliding with the trolley. The bottles and cans shook. Two packets of gingerbread biscuits rocketed onto the floor. The man was terrified. But why?

"Paris is so beautiful in the spring," the old lady said. She'd obviously seen the effect that

Tim was having on the steward and perhaps she was trying to change the subject before the poor man had a heart attack. "You must make sure you take a stroll on the Champs Elysées … if you have the time."

"How much do I owe you for the coffee?" the American asked.

"Four euros, monsieur…" The steward reached down and picked up the biscuits. The way he took the money and moved off, he could have been trying to get to Paris ahead of the train. I guessed he wanted to get away from us as fast as he could. And I was right. He didn't even stop to offer anyone else in the carriage a coffee. He simply disappeared. Later, when I went to the loo, I saw the trolley standing on its own in the passageway.

Twenty minutes after we'd entered the tunnel, the train burst out again. There was nothing to show that we'd left one country and entered another. The French cows grazing in the fields looked just the same as the English ones on the other side. An official came past, looking at passports. Erica Nice looked at Tim as if puzzled in some way and went back to her knitting. Jed returned to his magazine. We didn't speak for the rest of the journey.

We arrived at the Gare du Nord about an hour later. As everyone struggled with their luggage, Tim gazed at the name. "When do we arrive in Paris?" he asked.

"Tim, this is Paris," I told him. "The Gare du Nord means north station. There are lots of stations in the city."

"I hope you have a lovely time," Erica Nice said. She had an old carpet-bag. It was big enough to hold a carpet – and maybe that was what she had been knitting. She winked at Tim. "Good luck with the case, mon ami!"

Meanwhile, the Texan had grabbed a leather briefcase. He nodded at us briefly and joined the queue for the exit. Tim and I retrieved our two bags and a few moments later we were standing on the platform, wondering which way to go.

"We'd better find the Metro," I said. Bestlé had given us some spending money for the weekend but I didn't think it would be enough for us to travel everywhere by taxi.

Tim shook his head. "Forget the metro, Nick," he said. "Let's take the tube."

I didn't even bother to argue. I knew a little French – I'd been learning it from a little Frenchman who taught at our school – and I knew, for example, that Metro was the French word for tube train. On the other hand, I didn't know the French for idiot, which was the English word for Tim. I picked up the bags and prepared to follow him when suddenly we found ourselves interrupted.

It was Marc Chabrol. The French steward had reappeared and was standing in front of us, blocking our way. He was terrified. I could see it in his bulging eyes, the sweat on his cheeks, the yellow and black bow tie which had climbed halfway up his neck.

"I have to talk to you, Monsieur," he rasped. He was speaking in English, the words as uncomfortable in his mouth as somebody else's false teeth. "Tonight. At eleven o'clock. There is a café in the sixth *arrondisement*. It is called La Palette..."

"That's very nice of you," Tim said. He seemed to think that Chabrol was inviting us out for a drink.

"Beware of the mad American!" The steward whispered the words as if he were too afraid to speak them aloud. "The mad American...!"

He was about to add something but then his face changed again. He seemed to freeze as if his worst nightmare had just come true. I glanced left and right but if there was someone he had recognized in the crowd, I didn't see them. *"Oh mon Dieu!"* he whispered. He seized Tim's hand and pressed something into the palm. Then he turned and staggered away.

Tim opened his hand. He was holding a small blue envelope with a gold star printed on the side. I recognized it at once. It was a sachet of sugar from the train. "What was all that about?" Tim asked.

I took the sugar and examined it. I thought

he might have written something on it – a tele-phone number or something. But it was just a little bag of sugar. I slipped it into my back pocket. "I don't know…" I said. And I didn't. Why should the steward have left us with a spoonful of sugar? Why did he want to meet us later that night? What was going on?

"Funny people, the French," Tim said.

Ten minutes later, we were still at the Gare du Nord. The money that Bestlé had given us was in English pounds and pence. We needed euros and that meant queuing up at the Bureau de Change. The queue was a long one and it seemed to be moving at a rate of one euro per hour.

We had just reached the window when we heard the scream.

It was like no sound I had ever heard, thin and high and horribly final. The station was huge and noisy but the scream cut through the crowd like a scalpel. Everybody stopped and turned to see where it had come from. Even Tim heard it. "Oh dear," he said. "It sounds like someone has stepped on a cat."

Tim changed thirty pounds, and taking the money we moved in the direction of the Metro. Already a police car had arrived and several uniformed gendarmes were hurrying towards the trains. I strained to hear what the crowd was saying. They were speaking French, of course. That didn't make it any easier.

"What's happened?"

"It's terrible. Somebody has fallen under a train."

"It was a steward. He was on the train from London. He fell off a platform."

"Is he hurt?"

"He's dead. Crushed by a train."

I heard all of it. I understood some of it. I didn't like any of it. A steward? Off the London train? Somehow I didn't need to ask his name.

"Tim," I asked. "What's the French for murder?"

Tim shrugged. "Why do you want to know?"

"I don't know." I stepped onto the escalator and allowed it to carry me down. "I've just got a feeling it's something we're going to need."

LE CHAT GRIS

Le Chat Gris was in the Latin quarter, a dark, busy area on the south side of the River Seine. Here the streets were full of students and the smell of cheap food. It was a small, narrow building, wedged between an art gallery and a café. A metal cat, more rusty than grey, hung over the main entrance and there were brightly coloured flowers in the front windows. On closer inspection they turned out to be made of plastic.

The reception area was so small that if you went in too quickly you'd be out the other side. There was a receptionist standing behind the desk which was just as well as there wasn't enough room for a chair. He was an old man, at least sixty, with a crumpled face and something terribly wrong with his eyes. When he looked at our passports he had to hold them up beside his ear. He took our names, then sent us to a room on the fifth floor. Fortunately there was a lift but it wasn't much bigger than a telephone box. Tim and I stood shoulder to shoulder with our cases as it creaked and trembled slowly up. Next time, I decided, I'd take the stairs.

The truth was that Bestlé hadn't been too generous with the accommodation. Our room was built into the roof with wooden beams that sloped down at strange angles. It made me think of the Hunchback of Notre Dame. You needed a hunched back to avoid hitting your head on the ceiling. There were two beds, a single window with a view over the other rooftops, a chest of drawers and a bathroom too small to take a bath.

"Which bed do you want?" I asked.

"This one!" Tim threw himself onto the bed next to the window. There was a loud "ping" as several of the springs snapped. I sat down, more carefully, on the other bed. It felt like the duvet wasn't just filled with goose feathers, but they'd also left in half the goose.

We dumped our luggage and went out. This was, after all, Thursday morning and we only had until Sunday afternoon. Back in the reception area, the receptionist was talking to a new arrival. This was a square-shouldered man with narrow eyes and black, slicked-back hair. He was wearing an expensive, charcoal grey suit. Both of them stopped when they saw us.

I dropped the key with a clunk.

"*Merci,*" I said.

Neither of the men said anything. Maybe it was my accent.

There was a mirror next to the front door and but for that I wouldn't have noticed what happened next. But as Tim and I made our way out, the man in the grey suit reached out and took my key, turning it round so that he could read the number. He was interested in us. That was for sure. His eyes, empty of emotion, were still scrutinizing us as the door swung shut and we found ourselves in the street.

First the death of the steward on the train. Then the last whispered warning: "*Beware the mad American!*" And now this. There was a nasty smell in the air and already I knew it wasn't just French cheese.

"Which way, Nick?" Tim was waiting for me, holding a camera. He had already taken three photographs of the hotel, a streetlamp and a post-box and he was waiting for me in the morning sunlight. I wondered if he had remembered to put in a film.

I thought for a moment. I was probably being stupid. We were here in Paris for the weekend and nothing was going to happen. I couldn't even be sure that it really was Marc Chabrol who had fallen under the train. "Let's try down there," I said, pointing down the street.

"Good idea," Tim agreed as he turned the other way.

What can I tell you about Paris? I'm no travel writer. I'm not crazy about writing and I can't usually afford to travel. But anyway…

Paris is a big city full of French people. It's a lot prettier than London and for that matter so are the people. They're everywhere: in the street-side cafés, sipping black coffee from thimble-sized cups, strolling along the Seine in their designer sunglasses, snapping at each other on the bridges through eighteen inches of the latest Japanese lens. The streets are narrower than in London and looking at the traffic you get the feeling that war has broken out. There are cars parked everywhere. On the streets and on the pavements. Actually, it's hard to tell which cars are parked and which ones are just stuck in the traffic jams. But the strange thing is that nobody seems to be in a hurry. Life is just a big jumble that moves along at its own pace and if you're in a hurry to leave then maybe you should never have come there in the first place.

That first day, Tim and I did the usual tourist things. We went up the Eiffel Tower. Tim fainted. So we came down again. We went to the cathedral of Notre Dame and I took a picture of Tim and another of a gargoyle. I just hoped that when I got them developed I'd remember which was which. We went up the Champs Elysées and down the Jardin des Tuileries. By lunch-time, my stomach was rumbling. So, more worryingly, were my feet.

We had an early supper at a brasserie over-looking another brasserie. That's another thing about Paris. There are brasseries everywhere. Tim ordered two ham sandwiches, a beer for him and a Coke for me. Then I ordered them again using words the waiter understood. The sandwiches arrived: twenty centimetres of bread, I noticed, but only ten centimetres of ham.

"This is the life, eh, Nick?" Tim sighed as he sipped his beer.

"Yes, Tim," I said. "And this is the bill."

Tim glanced at it and swallowed his beer the wrong way. "Ten euros!" he exclaimed. "That's ... that's...!" He frowned. "How much is that?"

"A euro's worth about seven old francs," I explained. "It's about seventy pence. So the bill is about seven quid."

Tim shook his head. "I hate this new money," he said.

"I know," I agreed. "Because you haven't got any."

We were walking back in the direction of the hotel when it happened. We were in one of those quiet, antique streets near the Seine when two men appeared, blocking our way. The first was in his forties, tall and slim, wearing a white linen suit that was so crumpled and dirty, it hung off him like a used paper bag. He was one of the ugliest men I had ever seen. He had green eyes, a small nose and a mouth like a knife wound. None of these were in quite the right place. It was as if his whole face had been drawn by a six-year-old child.

His partner was about twenty years younger with the body of an ape and, if the dull glimmer in his eyes was anything to go by, a brain to match. He was wearing jeans and a leather jacket and smoking a cigarette. I guessed he was a body-builder. He had muscles bulging everywhere and a neck that somehow managed to be wider than his head. His hair was blonde and greasy. He had fat lips and a tiny beard sprouting out of the middle of his chin.

"Good evening," White Suit said in perfect English. His voice came out like a whisper from a punctured balloon. "My name is Bastille. Jacques Bastille. My friend's name is Lavache. I wonder if I might speak with you."

"If you want to know the way, don't ask us!" Tim replied. "We're lost too."

"I'm not lost. Oh, no." Bastille smiled, revealing teeth the colour of French mustard. "No. But I want to know what he told you. I want to know what you know."

Tim turned to me, puzzled.

"What exactly do you mean?" I asked.

"The steward on the train. What did he tell you?" There was a pause. Then ... "Lavache!"

Bastille nodded and his partner produced what looked like a little model of that famous statue, the Venus de Milo. You know the one. The naked woman with no arms that stands somewhere in the Louvre.

"No thank you," Tim began. "We're not..."

Lavache pressed a button and ten centimetres of razor-sharp metal sprang out of the head of the statue. It was a neat trick. I don't think the real statue ever did that.

Tim stared at it.

"Where is it?" Bastille demanded.

"Your friend's holding it in his hand!" Tim gasped.

"Not the knife! *Sacré bleu!* Are all the English such idiots? I am talking about the object. The item that you were given this morning at the Gare du Nord."

"I wasn't given anything!" Tim wailed.

"It's true," I said, even though I knew that it wasn't.

Bastille blinked heavily. "You're lying."

"No, we're not," Tim replied. "Cross my heart and hope to..."

"Tim!" I interrupted.

"Kill them both!" Bastille snapped.

They really did mean to kill us there and then in that quiet Paris street. Lavache lifted the knife, his stubby fingers curving around the

34

base, a bead of saliva glistening at the corner of his mouth. I glanced back, wondering if we could run. But it was hopeless. We'd be cut down before we could take a step.

"The older one first," Bastille commanded.

"That's him!" Tim said, pointing at me.

"Tim!" I exclaimed.

The knife hovered between us.

But then suddenly a party of American tourists turned the corner – about twenty of them, following a guide who was holding an umbrella with a Stars and Stripes attached to the tip. They were jabbering excitedly as they descended on us. There was nothing Bastille and Lavache could do. Suddenly they were surrounded, and realizing this was our only chance I grabbed hold of Tim and moved away, keeping a wall of American tourists between us and our attackers. Only when we'd come to the top of the street where it joined the wide and busy Boulevard St Michel did we break away and run.

But the two killers weren't going to let us get away quite so easily. I glanced back and saw them pushing their way through the crowd. Bastille shoved out a hand and one of the tourists, an elderly woman, shrieked and fell backwards into a fountain. Several of the other tourists stopped and took photographs of her. Bastille stepped into the road. A car swerved to avoid him and crashed into the front of a restaurant. Two lobsters and a plateful of mussels were sent flying. Someone screamed.

It still wasn't dark. The streets were full of people on their way to restaurants, too wrapped up in their own affairs to notice two English visitors running for their lives. I had no idea where I was going and I wasn't going to stop and ask for directions. I grabbed Tim again and steered him up an alleyway with dozens more restaurants on both sides. A waiter in a long white apron, carrying several trays laden with plates and glasses, stepped out in front of me. There was no way I could avoid him. There was a strangled cry, then a crash.

"Excusez-moi!" Tim burbled.

Fortunately, I didn't know enough French to understand the waiter's reply.

The alleyway brought us back to the Seine. I could see Notre Dame in the distance. Only a few hours before we had been standing on one of its towers, enjoying the view. How could our holiday have become a nightmare so quickly?

"This way, Tim!" I shouted.

I pulled him across a busy street, cars screeching to a halt, horns blaring. A gendarme turned round to face us, a whistle clenched between his teeth, his hands scrabbling for his gun. I swear he would have shot us except that we were already on the other side of the road and a few seconds later Bastille had reached him, brutally pushing him out of the way. The unfortunate gendarme spun round and collided with a cyclist. Both of them collapsed in a tangle of rubber and steel. The last I saw of the gendarme, he had got back to his feet and was shouting at us, making a curious, high-pitched noise. Evidently he had swallowed his whistle which had now got lodged in his throat.

The river was now right in front of us with a pedestrian bridge leading over to the other side. Bastille and Lavache were already crossing the road, blocked for a moment by a bus that had slipped in between them and us.

"The river!" I said.

Tim reached into his pocket and took out his camera.

"No!" I yelled. "I don't want you to photograph it! I want us to cross it!"

We ran onto the bridge, but I hadn't taken more than a few steps before I saw that we'd made a bad mistake. The bridge was closed. There was a tall barrier running across the middle of it with a MEN AT WORK sign – but no sign at all of any men actually at work. They had left their tools, though. There was a wheelbarrow, a pile of steel girders, a cement mixer ... even if we could have climbed over the fence it would have been hard to get through.

"We've got to go back!" I shouted.

But it was too late. Bastille and Lavache had already arrived at the entrance to the bridge and were moving more slowly, both of them smiling. They knew they had us trapped. Lavache had his knife out. It was difficult to hear with the noise of the traffic, but I think he was humming.

We couldn't go back. We couldn't climb the fence. If we jumped over the side, we'd probably drown. This was only March and the water would be ice-cold. Just twenty metres separated us from the two Frenchmen. There was nothing we could do.

And that was when I saw the boat. It was what they called a Bateau Mouche, one of those long, elegant boats with glass windows and ceilings that carry tourists up and down the river throughout the day and night. This one was full of people enjoying a dinner and dance. I heard the music drifting up to us. They were playing a waltz, the "Blue Danube". A strange choice considering they were on the Seine. Already the boat was slipping under the bridge. Another few seconds and it would have disappeared down towards the Eiffel Tower.

"Jump, Tim!" I ordered.

"Right, Nick!" Tim jumped up and down on the spot.

"No. I mean – jump off the bridge!"

"What?" Tim looked at me as if I was mad. Bastille was only five steps away from us now. I ran to the edge of the bridge, hoisted myself up and jumped. Tim did the same, a few seconds behind me. I caught a glimpse of Bastille, staring at us, his face twisted between anger and amazement. Then I was falling through space with the river, the bridge and the boat corkscrewing around me. I thought I might have mistimed it but then my feet hit something and I crashed onto the deck. I was lucky. I had hit the front of the boat where there was a sheet of tarpaulin stretched out amid a tangle of ropes. It broke my fall.

Tim was less fortunate. He had jumped a few seconds after me, allowing the boat to travel a few metres further forward. I heard the glass shatter as he went feet first through the glass roof. There were more screams and the music stopped. I pulled myself up and gazed groggily through a window. Tim had landed on one of the tables and was lying there, sprawled out, surrounded by broken plates and glasses and with what looked like a whole roast duck in his lap.

"Que fais-tu? Qu'est-ce que se passe?"

A man in a blue uniform had appeared on the deck. He was staring at me in horror. It was the captain of the Bateau Mouche. There were a couple of waiters with him. I didn't even struggle as the three of them grabbed hold of me. I wondered if they were going to lock me up or throw me over the side. Certainly it didn't look as if they were going to invite me in for a dance and something to eat.

I twisted round and took one last look back at the bridge. Bastille and Lavache were leaning over the side, watching, and as I was dragged inside they vanished, swallowed up in the gathering gloom.

DOWN AND OUT

You won't meet many thirteen-year-olds who have been locked up in prisons on both sides of the Channel, but I'm one of them. I did time in Strangeday Hall, sharing a cell with Johnny Powers, England's public enemy number one*, and here I was in prison in Paris, this time with Tim. It was half past nine in the evening. We'd been given dinner – bread and water – but the fact that it was French bread and Perrier didn't make it taste any better.

Miraculously, neither Tim nor I had been hurt jumping from the bridge. The captain had locked us both up in the kitchen on board the ship and by the time we docked, the police were already waiting. I suppose he must have radioed on ahead. I hadn't tried to argue as we were thrown into the back of a van and driven at high speed through the streets of Paris.

* See *Public Enemy Number Two*

Nobody spoke English and even if they had they wouldn't have believed us. I assumed they'd call the British consul or someone. I would leave the explanations until then.

Neither of us had said anything for a while but at last Tim broke the silence. "That's the last time I buy a Bestlé yoghurt," he muttered.

"It wasn't their fault, Tim," I said, although I knew how he felt. We hadn't even been in Paris one day and we'd witnessed one murder, been chased by two killers and were now locked up ourselves. It was probably just as well that we weren't planning to stay a whole week. "I just wish I knew what it was all about," I added.

"They tried to kill us, Nick," Tim explained. "They nearly *did* kill us!"

"I noticed, Tim. But why?"

Tim thought for a moment. "Perhaps they don't like foreigners?" he suggested.

"No. They were looking for something. Something they thought we had." I already knew it had to be tied in with Marc Chabrol, the steward we had met at the Gare du Nord, and the sachet of sugar he had given us. But what could be so important about a packet of sugar? It was still in my back pocket. I reached in and took it out. "This is what they were after," I said.

"Sugar?"

"Unless there's something else inside…"

42

I was about to open it there and then but at that moment the door opened and a young policeman with close-cropped hair and glasses walked in. I slipped the sachet back into my pocket. I could always examine it later.

"This way, please," the policeman said.

He led us back out and down a corridor, then into an interrogation room that smelled of cigarette smoke. There was a table and three chairs but nothing else, not even a window. A naked light bulb hung on a short flex from the ceiling. The policeman gestured and we all sat down.

"You are English," he said.

"That's right," I said. The man obviously had a first-class brain.

"This is an outrage!" Tim exclaimed. "You can't keep us here. I demand to speak to the British ambassador! If the British ambassador is busy, I'll speak to his wife."

The policeman leaned forward. "First of all, monsieur, I can keep you here for as long as I wish," he said. "And secondly, I doubt very much that the British ambassador would be interested in you. Or his wife!"

"Why wouldn't he be interested in his wife?" Tim asked.

The policeman ignored him. "You and your small brother have caused great damage to one of our Bateaux Mouches," he went on. "It is most fortunate that nobody was injured. I wish to know why the two of you jumped off the bridge. You were trying to commit suicide, perhaps? Or could it have been a joke?"

"It was no joke," I said. "There were two men trying to kill us…"

The policeman looked at me in disbelief.

"It's true," I went on. "They said their names were Bastille and Lavache. They had a knife…"

"Tell me your names," the policeman commanded. He took out a notebook and prepared to write.

"I'm Tim Diamond," Tim said. "You may have heard of me."

"No, monsieur…"

"Well, I'm a well-known detective back in London." Tim pointed at the notebook. "That's the capital of England," he added, helpfully.

The policeman paused and took a deep breath. He was getting older by the minute. "I am aware of that," he said. "May I ask, what is your business here in Paris?"

"Of course you can ask!" Tim said.

The policeman groaned. "What is your business?" he demanded.

"We're on holiday," I told him. "We only arrived today. We're staying in Le Chat Gris in the Latin quarter…"

The policeman looked at me strangely, as if he were seeing me properly for the first time.

"Le Chat Gris..." he repeated. He closed the notebook. "Could you please wait here for a minute."

He stood up and left the room.

In fact it was ten minutes before he returned. The moment he walked in, I noticed there was something different about him. He was brisk, emotionless. And when he spoke, he did his best not to meet our eyes. "I have spoken with my superior officer," he said. "And he says that you are free to go!"

"How can we be free to go when we're locked up in here?" Tim asked.

"No, no, no, monsieur. He says that you may leave."

"They're unlocking the door and letting us out," I explained.

"As far as we are concerned, this incident is closed." The policeman did the same to his notebook.

"What about Bastille and Lavache?" I asked.

"We have no record of these men. It is our view that they do not exist!"

"What?"

"You jump off the bridge for a joke or maybe as a game and you make up the story of the killers to explain your actions. That is the view of my Superintendent."

"Well, he can't be as super as all that," I growled.

But there was no point arguing. For whatever their reasons, the French police had decided to let us go. As far as I was concerned, I just wanted to get out of jail. And out of Paris too, for that matter. I'd only been there for a day but so far our visit had been less fun than a French lesson – and twice as dangerous.

"Let's go, Tim," I said.

And we went.

It was almost eleven o'clock by the time we got back to the Latin quarter, but the night wasn't over yet. Tim wanted to stop for a beer and I was still anxious to open the packet of sugar that was burning a hole in my back pocket. We looked for a café and quite by coincidence found ourselves outside an old-fashioned, artistic sort of place whose name I knew. It was La Palette, the very same café where the train steward, Marc Chabrol, had asked us to meet.

He wasn't there, of course. Right now, if Chabrol was sipping coffee, it was with two wings and a halo. But there was someone there that we recognized. He was sitting out in the front, smoking a cigar, gazing into the night sky. There was no way I'd forget the hat. It was Jed Mathis, the businessman we had met on the train.

Tim saw him. "It's Ned," he said.

"You mean Jed," I said.

"Why don't we join him?"

"Forget it!" I grabbed Tim and we walked forward, continuing towards our hotel.

"But Nick! He paid for the drinks on the train. Maybe he'd buy me a beer."

"Yes, Tim. But think for a minute. What's he doing at La Palette?" I looked at my watch. It was eleven o'clock exactly. "It could just be a coincidence. But maybe he's waiting for someone. Maybe he's waiting for us! Don't you remember what Marc Chabrol said?"

"He asked us if we wanted to buy a KitKat."

"Yes. But after that. In the station, he warned us about someone who he called 'the mad American'. Jed Mathis is American! He said he was from Texas."

"You think Mathis killed Chabrol?"

"Mathis was on the train. And Chabrol ended up underneath it. I don't know. But I don't think we should hang around and have drinks with him. I think we should go home!"

We hurried on. Le Chat Gris loomed up ahead of us, but before we got there I noticed something else.

There was a man standing opposite the hotel. It was hard to recognize him because he was holding a camera up to his face, taking a picture. I heard the click of the button and the whir as the film wound on automatically. He wasn't a tourist. That much was certain. Not unless his idea of a holiday snap was two

English tourists about to check out. Because the photograph he had taken had been of us. There could be no doubt about it. I could feel the telephoto lens halfway up my nose.

He lowered the camera and now I recognized the man. He had been standing in the reception area that morning when we left: a dark-haired man in a grey suit.

Marc Chabrol, the steward.

Bastille and Lavache.

And now this.

Just what was happening in Paris and why did it all have to happen to us?

A car suddenly drew up, a blue Citroën. The man with the camera got in and a moment later they were roaring past us. I just caught a glimpse of the driver, smoking a cigarette with one hand, steering with the other. Then they were gone.

Tim had already walked into the hotel. Feeling increasingly uneasy, I followed him in.

We took the key from the squinting receptionist and took the stairs back to the top of the hotel. There were a lot of them and the stairway was so narrow that the walls brushed both my shoulders as I climbed. Finally we got to the last floor. Tim stopped for breath. Then he unlocked our door.

Our room had been torn apart. The sheets had been pulled off the bed and the mattress slashed open, springs and enough hair to

48

cover a horse tumbling out onto the floor. Every drawer had been opened, upturned and smashed. The carpet had been pulled up and the curtains down. Tim's jackets and trousers had been scattered all over the room. And I mean scattered. We found one arm on a window-sill, one leg in the shower, a single pocket under what was left of the bed. Our suitcases had been cut open and turned inside out. We'd need another suitcase just to carry the old ones down to the bin.

Tim gazed at the destruction. "I can't say I think too much of room service, Nick," he said.

"This isn't room service, Tim!" I exploded. "The room's been searched!"

"What do you think they were looking for?"

"This!" I took out the packet of sugar. Once again I was tempted to open it – but this wasn't the right time. "This is the only thing Chabrol gave us back at the station. It must be the object that Bastille was talking about." I slid it back into my pocket, then thought again. It seemed that Bastille was determined to get his hands on the sugar. I wouldn't be safe carrying it. It was better to leave it in the hotel room. After all, they'd already searched the place once. It was unlikely they'd think of coming back.

I looked around, then slid the sugar into the

toilet-roll in the bathroom, inside the card-board tube. Nobody would notice it there and the police could pick it up later. Because that was the next step.

"We've got to call the police," I said.

"We've just come from the police," Tim reminded me.

"I know. But if they see our room, they've got to believe us. And as soon as they're here, I'll show them the packet. Maybe they'll be able to work the whole thing out."

I looked for the telephone and eventually found it – or what was left of it. You'd have to be an expert at electronics or at least very good at jigsaws to use it again.

"Why don't we talk to the man downstairs?" Tim asked.

I thought of the squinting receptionist. Only that morning he'd been talking to the man in the grey suit, the one who'd just taken our photograph.

"I don't trust him," I said. At that moment I wouldn't have trusted my own mother.

Tim held up a short-sleeved shirt. It had been a long-sleeved shirt when he had packed it. He looked as if he was going to burst into tears. At least he could use the rest of the shirt as a handkerchief if he did.

"Let's go back down, Tim," I said. "We can call the police from the lobby. I noticed a phone booth."

"What's the French for 999?" Tim asked.

"17," I replied. I'd seen it written next to the phone.

But the phone in the hotel was out of order. There was a sign on the window reading *"Hors de service"*. I translated for Tim and he went over to the receptionist. "We want to call the police," he said.

"Please?" The receptionist narrowed his eye. I think he would have liked to have narrowed both his eyes, but the one on the left wasn't working.

"No," Tim explained. "Police." He saluted and bent his knees, doing an imitation of a policeman. The receptionist stared at him as if he had gone mad.

"Les flics," I said.

"Ah!" The receptionist nodded. Then he leant forward and pointed. "You go out the door. You turn left. Then you take the first turning left again," he growled. He actually spoke pretty good English even if the words had trouble getting past his throat. "There's a police station just at the next corner."

We left the hotel, turned left and then immediately left again. We found ourselves in a narrow alleyway that twisted its way through the shadows before coming to a brick wall.

"This is wrong," I said.

"You don't want to go to the police anymore?" Tim asked.

51

"No, Tim. I still want to go to the police but this is the wrong way. It's a dead-end."

"Maybe we have to climb over the wall."

"I don't think so…"

I was getting worried. After everything that had happened to us so far, the last place I wanted to be was a dead-end … or anywhere else with the word "dead" in it. And I was right. There was a sudden squeal as a van appeared racing towards us. The squeal, incidentally, came from Tim. The van was reversing. For a moment I thought it was going to crush us, but it stopped, just centimetres away. The back doors flew open. Two men got out.

Everything was happening too quickly. I couldn't even tell who the men were or if I had seen them before. I saw one of them lash out and Tim spun round, crumpling to the ground. Then it was my turn. Something hard hit me on the back of the head. My legs buckled. I fell forward and one of the men must have caught me as I felt myself being half-pushed, half-carried into the back of the van.

Tim was next to me. "Some holiday!" he said.

Then either they hit me again or they hit him. Or maybe they hit both of us. Either way, I was out cold.

PARIS BY NIGHT

I knew I was in trouble before I even opened my eyes. For a start, I was sitting up. If everything that had happened up until now had been a horrible dream – which it should have been – I would be lying in my nice warm bed in Camden with the kettle whistling in the kitchen and maybe Tim doing the same in the bath. But not only was I sitting in a hard, wooden chair, my feet were tied together with something that felt suspiciously like parcel tape and my hands were similarly bound behind my back. When I did finally open my eyes, it only got worse. Tim was next to me looking pale and confused ... by which I mean even more confused than usual. And Bastille and Lavache were sitting opposite us, both of them smoking.

The four of us were in a large, empty room that might once have been the dining-room of a grand château but was now empty and dilapidated. The floor was wooden and the walls white plaster, with no pictures or decorations. A broken chandelier hung from the ceiling. In fact quite a lot of the ceiling was hanging from the ceiling. Half of it seemed to be peeling off.

I had no idea how much time had passed since they'd knocked us out and bundled us into the back of a delivery van. An hour? A week? I couldn't see my watch – it was pinned somewhere behind me, along with the wrist it was on – so I twisted round and looked out of the window. The glass was so dust-covered that I could barely see outside, but from the light I would have said it was early evening. If so, we had been unconscious for about fifteen hours! I wondered where we were. Somewhere in the distance I thought I heard singing, the sound of a choir. But the music was foreign – and not French. It sounded vaguely religious, which made me think of churches. And that made me think of funerals. I just hoped they weren't singing for us.

"Good evening," Bastille muttered. He hadn't changed out of the dirty linen suit he had been wearing when we met him the day before. It was so crumpled now that I wondered if he had slept in it.

"What time is it?" Tim asked.

"It is time for you to talk!" Bastille blew a cloud of smoke into Tim's face.

54

Tim coughed. "You know those things can damage your health!" he remarked.

Not quickly enough, I thought. But I said nothing.

"It is *your* health that should concern you, my friend," Bastille replied.

"I'm perfectly well, thank you," Tim said.

"I mean – your health if you fail to tell us what we want to know!" Bastille's green eyes flared. He was even uglier when he was angry. "You have put us to a great deal of trouble," he went on. "We've searched you and this morning we searched your room. Are you going to tell us where it is?"

"It's on the top floor of the hotel!" Tim exclaimed.

"Not the room!" Bastille swore and choked on his cigarette. "I am talking about the packet that you were given by Marc Chabrol."

"The ex-steward," Lavache added. He giggled, and, looking at his ape-like hands, I suddenly knew how Chabrol had managed to "fall" under a train.

I'd said nothing throughout all this. I was just glad that I'd decided not to bring the packet with us. The two men must have searched Tim and me while we were unconscious. They had found nothing and it looked like they weren't going to go back and search the hotel room a second time.

"He gave us a cup of coffee," Tim was

saying. "But we drank it. Unless you're talking about … wait a minute…"

"Who *are* you people?" I cut in. I didn't want him to say any more. So long as we had the sachet, they wouldn't kill us. They needed to know where it was. But the moment they heard it was hidden in the toilet, we were dead. That much was certain. I would just have to keep them talking and hope for the best. "Look…" I went on. "The steward didn't give us anything. We're just here on holiday."

"*Non, non, non!*" Bastille shook his head. "Do not try lying to me, *mon petit ami*. I know that your brother is a private detective. I also know that he was sent to Paris by Interpol. I know that he is working on a special assigment." His face turned ugly, which, with his face, wasn't difficult. "Now I want you to tell me how much you know and who gave you your information."

"But I don't know anything!" Tim wailed.

He'd never spoken a truer word in his life. Tim knew nothing about any special assignment. He'd have had trouble telling anyone his own shoe size. And he also hadn't realized that this was all his fault. If only he'd kept his mouth shut on the train! He'd told Jed Mathis and the old woman that he was working for Interpol. Could one of them have passed it on? Jed Mathis…?

Beware the mad American…

It was too late to worry about that. I realized that Tim was still talking. He had told them everything. The competition on the yoghurt pot. The free weekend. The truth.

"He's right," I admitted. "We're just tourists. We're not working for anyone."

"It was a strawberry yoghurt!" Tim burbled. "Bestlé yoghurts. They're only eighty calories each..."

"We don't know anything!" I said.

Bastille and Lavache moved closer to each other and began to mutter in low, dark voices. I couldn't understand a word they were saying, but somehow I didn't like the sound of it. I tried to break free from the chair but it was useless. Things weren't looking good. By now they must have realized that they were wrong about us, that we were exactly what we said. But they weren't just going to order us a taxi and pretend the whole thing had never happened. As they're always saying in the old movies ... we knew too much. I still had no idea who they were or what they were doing, but we knew their names and had seen their faces. That was enough.

The two men straightened up. "We have decided that we believe you," Bastille said.

"That's terrific!" Tim exclaimed.

"So now we are going to kill you."

"Oh!" His face fell.

Lavache walked to the far side of the room

57

and I strained my neck to watch him. He reached out with both hands and suddenly a whole section of the wall slid to one side. I realized now that it wasn't a wall at all but a set of floor-to-ceiling doors. There was another room on the other side, filled with activity, and at that moment I realized what this was all about. Perhaps I should have guessed from the start.

Drugs.

The other room was a laboratory. I could see metal tables piled high with white powder. More white powder being weighed on complicated electronic scales. White powder being spooned into plastic bags. There were about half-a-dozen people working there, young men and women with dirty faces but pristine laboratory coats. They were handling the white powder in complete silence, as if they knew that it was death they were carrying in their hands and that if it heard them it would somehow find them out.

Lavache lumbered into the room, vanishing from sight. When he reappeared, he was holding something which he handed to Bastille. Right then I was more scared than I've ever been in my life, and you know me … I don't scare easily. But suddenly I remembered that I was thirteen years old, that I hadn't started shaving yet and that my mother (who'd been shaving for years) was thousands of miles away. I was so scared I almost wanted to cry.

Bastille was holding a bottle of pills.

He approached Tim first. "These are super-strength," he said. "I think five of them will be enough."

"No, thank you," Tim said. "I haven't got a headache."

"They're not headache pills, Tim," I said.

Bastille grabbed hold of Tim and forced his mouth open. He had counted five pills into the palm of his hand and I watched, powerless, as he forced them down Tim's throat. Then he turned and began to walk towards me.

"They don't taste very nice!" I heard Tim say, but then I'd gone crazy, rocking back and forth, yelling, kicking with my feet, trying to tear apart the parcel tape around my wrists. It was useless. I felt Lavache grab hold of my shoulders while at the same time, Bastille took hold of my chin. I don't know what was worse. Feeling his bony fingers against my face or knowing there was nothing I could do as he forced my mouth open. His right hand came up and the next moment there were four or five pills on my tongue. They had an evil taste. I drew a breath, meaning to spit them out, but his hand was already over my mouth, almost suffocating me. I screamed silently and felt the pills trickle down the back of my throat. I almost felt them drop into the pit of my stom-ach. Then Bastille pulled his hand clear and my head sank forward. I said nothing. I thought I was dead. I thought he had killed me.

Things happened very quickly after that. It seemed to me that the lights in the room had brightened and that somebody had turned up the heating. My eyes were hurting. And then the walls began to revolve, slowly at first, like the start of a ride at a funfair. But there was nothing fun about this. Drugs are poison and I was sure I had just been given a lethal overdose. I was sweating. I tried to speak but my tongue refused to move; anyway, my mouth was too dry.

I heard the parcel tape being ripped off and felt my hands come free. Lavache was standing behind me. I tried to look at him, but my head lolled uselessly. He pulled me off the chair and carried me outside. Bastille followed with Tim.

There was a white van waiting for us in an enclosed courtyard – we could have been anywhere. I looked back at the house we had just left. It was a grey building, three storeys high. Most of its paint had flaked off and there were scorch marks, as if it had been involved in a fire. About half the windows were shattered. Others had been bricked in. The place looked derelict. I guessed it was supposed to.

I was bundled into the van and the next moment the engine started up, roaring at me like a mechanical beast. I almost expected it to come bursting through the floor, to gobble me up. The noise hammered at my ears and I groaned. Tim was thrown in next to me. The doors slammed. My stomach heaved. We were off.

There was a small window set in the door and I managed to stagger over to it and pull myself onto my knees to look out. But it was hard to see anything. The world was spinning faster now, tilting from side to side. I just made out a series of letters in red neon, but it seemed to take me for ever to work out the three words they formed:

THE FRENCH CONFECTION

The van turned a corner and I lost my balance. Before I fell, I caught a glimpse of a blue star ... on a flag or perhaps on the side of a building. Then the sound of the van's engine rose up again and swallowed me. The floor hit me in the face. Or maybe it was me who had hit the floor. I no longer knew the difference.

The journey took an hour ... a month ... a year. I no longer had any idea. What was the stuff they had given me? Whatever it was, it was taking over, killing me. I could feel it happening, an inch at a time. The van stopped. Hands that no longer belonged to bodies pulled us out. Then the pavement slapped me in the face, there was another scream from the engine and suddenly I knew that we were alone.

"Tim...?" I gasped the word. But Tim was no longer there. He had turned into some horrible animal with sixteen eyes, tentacles and...

I forced myself to concentrate, knowing that it was the drug that was doing it to me. The image dissolved and there he was again. My brother.

"Nick..." He staggered to his feet. All three of them. Things weren't back to normal yet.

The sky changed from red to blue to yellow to green. I stood up as well.

"Must get help," I said.

Tim groaned.

We were back in the centre of Paris. It was late at night. And Paris had never looked like this before.

There was the Seine but the water had gone, replaced by red wine that glowed darkly in the moonlight. It was twisting its way underneath the bridges, but now that I looked more closely, I saw that they had changed too. They had become huge sticks of French bread. There was a sudden buzzing. A Bateau Mouche had suddenly sprouted huge blue wings and legs. It leapt out of the water and onto one of the bridges, tearing a great chunk out with a hideous, hairy mouth before spiralling away into the night.

The ground underneath my feet had gone

soft and I realized I was sinking into it. With a cry I lifted one foot and saw that the tar had melted and was dripping off my trainer. Except the tar was yellow, not black.

"It's cheese!" I shouted. And it was. The entire street had turned into cheese – soft, ripe, French cheese. I gasped for air, choking on the smell. At the same time, the cheese pulled me into it. Another few seconds and I would be sucked underneath the surface.

"Nick!" Tim called out.

And then the cheese was gone as he pointed with an arm that was now a mile long. There was a snail coming down the Boulevard. No ... not one snail but a thousand of them, each one the size of a house, slithering along ahead of the traffic, leaving a grey, slimy trail behind them. At one corner, the traffic lights had gone red and all the snails were squeaking at each other, a fantastic traffic jam of snails. At the same time, I heard what sounded like a gigantic burp and a frog, the size of a bus, bounded across my vision, leaping over a building. But the frog was missing its legs. It was supporting itself on giant crutches.

The world twisted, heaved, broke up and then reformed with all the pieces in different positions: a jigsaw in the hands of a destructive child.

Suddenly we were surrounded by grinning stone figures, jabbering and staring at us with empty stone eyes. I recognized them: the gargoyles from Notre Dame. There must have been a hundred of them. One of them was sitting on Tim's shoulder like a grey chimpanzee. But Tim didn't seem to have noticed it.

Light. Car lights. Everywhere. A horn sounded. I had stepped into the road – but it didn't matter because the cars were the size of matchboxes. They were all Citroëns. Every one of them. And they were being followed by cyclists. The Tour de France had come early that year. All the cyclists were smoking cigarettes.

Tim was clutching a streetlamp. Now he was wearing a striped jersey and a beret and there was a string of onions hanging from his side. *"Je suis,"* he said. *"Tu es, il est..."*

I opened my mouth to reply.

Crash! Crash! Crash!

I saw it before he did. Perhaps he didn't see it at all. Even now, with the drug pumping through my body, I knew that it wasn't real, that I was hallucinating. But it made no difference. As far as I was concerned, everything I saw was real. And if it was real, it could kill me. It could step on me. It could crush me.

The Eiffel Tower! On our first day in Paris we had crossed the city to visit it. Now the Eiffel Tower was coming to visit us. There it was, walking across Paris, swinging one iron foot, then the next, moving like some sort of giant, four-legged crab. One of its feet came down in a pancake stall. Wood shattered. Pancakes flew in all directions. Somebody screamed.

The cheese was getting softer. I was sinking into a boulevard of Brie, a dual carriageway of Camembert. The squirming yellow slipped round my waist, rose over my shoulder and twisted round my neck. I didn't even try to fight. I'd had enough. I waited for it to pull me under.

I thought I was going to die and if I'd waited another minute I might well have. But just then I heard what I thought was an owl, hooting in my ear. At the same time, I found myself staring at a face I knew. A dark-haired man in a grey-coloured suit. I became aware of a blue flashing light which either belonged to a dragon or a police car. I looked up and saw something driving out of the moon, flying through the sky towards me. An ambulance.

"Don't go to sleep!" a voice commanded. "Don't go to sleep! Don't go to sleep!"

But it was too late. I went to sleep.

For ever.

THE MAD AMERICAN

"You're lucky to be alive," the man said.

It was two days later. I don't want to tell you about those two days. I'd spent both of them in hospital in Paris and all I can say is, if you've ever had your stomach pumped, you'll know there are plenty of things you can do that are more fun. I don't remember much about the first day. The next day, I felt like a spin-drier that's been left on too long. All I'd eaten in the entire time was a little bread and water. Fortunately, the water didn't have bubbles. I don't think I could have managed the bubbles.

And now, here I was in the headquarters of Sûreté, the French police force. It's funny how police stations are the same the whole world over. This may have been grander and smarter than New Scotland Yard. The curtains were velvet and the pictures on the wall showed some grey-haired Frenchman in a suit rather than our own grey-haired Queen in a crown. But it still smelled the same.

Tim was sitting next to me. He was the colour of the yoghurt that had brought us here in the first place, with eyes like crushed strawberries. His hair was dishevelled and he looked like he hadn't slept in a month. I was going to say something but decided against it. I probably looked just as bad.

We were in the office of the Chief of Police – a man called Christien Moire. I knew because I'd seen the name and title on the door. It was on his desk too. Maybe he was worried he was going to forget it. He was the man in the grey suit whom I'd seen standing outside Le Chat Gris, the man who had been talking to the receptionist and who had later taken our photograph. Things were beginning to add up even if I still had no idea of the sum total.

"Another one hour and it would have been too late," Moire went on. He spoke English as if he had no idea what he was saying, lingering on every word. He had the sort of accent you get in bad television plays: *Anuzzer wan our an' eet would 'ave bin too late.* I hope you get the idea. "You were very lucky," he added.

"Sure," I muttered. "And we'd have been even luckier if you'd arrived a couple of hours before."

Moire shrugged. "I'm sorry," he said. But

his dark, empty eyes looked about as apologetic as two lumps of ice. "We had no idea you had been taken," he went on.

"Who are you?" Tim demanded. "You call yourself the Sûreté. But what exactly are you sure about?"

"The Sûreté," Moire repeated, "is the French police force. I am the head of a special unit fighting the traffic in …"

"…drugs." I completed the sentence.

"*Exactement.* I have to say that you and your brother seem to have turned up in the wrong place at the wrong time. If I hadn't been watching you…"

"You were at the hotel," I said. "I saw you outside. You had a camera…"

"Is that your hobby?" Tim asked. "Photography?"

Christien Moire stared at Tim through narrow eyes. He obviously hadn't ever met anyone like him before. "Le Chat Gris has been under surveillance," he said. "Perhaps I should explain…"

"Perhaps you should," I said.

Moire lit a Gauloise. It's a funny thing about the French. Not only do they all smoke, but they smoke the most horrible cigarettes in the world. Forget about the health warning on the packet. The smoke from Moire's cigarette was so thick, you could have printed it on that.

"For some time now," he began, "we have

been aware of a drug-smuggling operation. Somebody has been moving drugs to London … using the trains under the channel. We still don't know how they're doing it. We have searched the trains from top to bottom but we have found nothing. Worse still, we do not know who they are."

"Is there anything you *do* know?" I asked.

Moire glanced at me with unfriendly eyes. "We know only the code-name of the man behind the operation," he replied.

"The Mad American," I said.

That surprised Moire, but he tried not to show it. "The drugs arrive from Marseilles," he went on. "They are weighed and packaged somewhere in Paris. Then the Mad American arranges for them to be sent to London. We've been working with the English police to try to stop them. So far we have had no success in London. But in Paris we had one lucky break."

"Le Chat Gris," I said.

"Yes, we learned that the hotel is sometimes used by the Mad American. When dealers arrive from London to buy his drugs, that is where they stay. He meets them there. They pay him the money and then his two associates – Jacques Bastille and Luc Lavache – arrange for the drugs to be sent on the train."

"So *that's* why you photographed us!" I said. "You thought we'd come to Paris to buy drugs!"

"I know it sounds unlikely," Moire said. "An English kid and his idiotic brother –"

"Nick isn't idiotic!" Tim protested.

"We became interested in you the moment you reported that Bastille and Lavache had attempted to kill you," Moire went on. "I ordered the photograph to be taken so that we could check you against our criminal files."

"But if you thought we were criminals, why did you let us go in the first place?" I asked. It had puzzled me at the time, the policeman suddenly changing his mind and telling us we could leave.

"The answer to that is simple," Moire said. "We still had no idea what part you had to play in all this, but you had mentioned Le Chat Gris and that was enough. It was important that the Mad American should not be aware that the police were involved. I personally ordered your release, and at the same time I made sure that we kept you under – how do you say? – surveillance. This was very lucky for you, considering how things turned out."

"You were following us."

"Yes. I saw you go back to the hotel, and minutes later I saw the van with the two men who knocked you out and kidnapped you. We followed the van but unfortunately lost it in traffic…"

"…so you don't know where we were taken."

"No. But I knew that you were in danger and I had every gendarme in Paris looking out for you. One of them saw you and radioed HQ. By that time they had pumped you with enough drugs to kill a horse."

"Why would they want to kill a horse?" Tim asked.

Moire ignored him. "We only got to you in the nick of time. Another ten minutes, and the two of you would now be in Père Lachaise."

"You mean, another hotel," Tim said.

"No. Père Lachaise is a cemetery."

"OK. You saved us, Monsieur Moire," I said. "But now, if you don't mind, I'm heading back to the hotel, packing and leaving for London."

"That's right, Monsieur Loire," Tim agreed. "We're out of here!"

"I'm afraid not." Moire hadn't raised his voice. If anything, he had done the exact opposite. But that's the thing about the French. When they're being really nasty, they don't shout. They whisper. "You realize that I could have you arrested?" he asked.

I almost laughed. "What for?" I demanded.

"You were found in the middle of Paris, full of drugs," the police chief explained. He sounded almost reasonable. "Two English tourists who decided to experiment with these forbidden substances…"

"That's a complete lie!" I exclaimed.

"Yes!" Tim agreed. "We're not tourists!"

"And then there is the matter of the Bateau Mouche..." Moire continued. "You jumped off a bridge, endangering the lives of the people on the boat. This could also prove to be drug-related."

"What do you want, Moire?" I demanded.

Moire leaned forward. His face could have been carved out of stone. Even the cigarette smoke seemed to have solidified. "There are two things we wish to find out," he said. "First, who is the Mad American?"

"Why don't you ask Bastille and Lavache?" I demanded.

"They wouldn't tell us anything. And if we did arrest them, it would only let their boss know that we were getting close ... and that would ruin everything. The second thing we wish to know is, how are they smuggling the drugs across the Channel? As I have told you, we have searched the train many times ... but with no success. These packets of white powder – they must be somewhere. But..." He smacked his forehead with the palm of his hand. "It is infuriating!"

"What do you want us to do?" I asked.

"I want you to go back to the hotel," Moire replied. "It will be as if nothing has happened."

"Why?"

"Because you can be useful to me ... on the

inside. My men will continue to watch you. You'll be completely safe. But maybe you can find the answers to the questions. And if there is anything to report…"

"Forget it!" I snapped.

"Right!" Tim nodded. "Bestlé only paid for four days. We can't possibly afford it."

"Bestlé?" For the first time Moire looked puzzled. "Who is Bestlé?"

"It doesn't matter," I replied. "We're British citizens. You can't blackmail us!"

"You don't think so?" Moire almost smiled. "You are Europeans now, my friend. And if you don't do exactly as I tell you, let me assure you that you will be spending a great deal of time inside a European jail."

I wanted to argue, but I could see there was no point. The last person to argue with Christien Moire probably found himself with a one-way ticket to Devil's Island.

He knew he'd beaten me. "Go back to Le Chat Gris and wait for further instructions," he said. "Don't worry about the bill. I will see to it."

"And what if we get killed?" I asked.

"My department will pay for the funeral too."

I sank back in my chair. There was nothing I could say. Not in French. Not in English. It really wasn't fair.

*   *   *

73

And that was how we found ourselves, a few hours later, back in our room at Le Chat Gris. As I'd walked back into the hotel, I'd known how those French aristocrats must have felt as they took their last steps towards the guillotine. The receptionist had almost fallen off his chair when he saw us and he'd been on the telephone before we'd reached the lift. The Mad American would have presumed we were dead. Now he'd know he was wrong. How long would it take him to correct his mistake?

Tim sat down on the bed. He was actually looking quite cheerful, which made me feel even worse. "Maybe this isn't so bad, Nick," he said.

"Tim!" I cried. "How bad can it get?"

"We're working for the French police now," he said. "This could be good for business! *Tim Diamond Inc … London and Paris.* That'll look good on the door."

"It'll look even better on your gravestone," I said. "Don't you understand, Tim?" We're not working for anyone! Christien Moire was lying through his teeth!"

"You mean … he isn't a policeman?"

"Of course he's a policeman. But he doesn't want us to work for him. He's using us!" I'd taken a guidebook of Paris out of my case. Now I sat down next to Tim. "Moire wants to find out the identity of the Mad American," I explained. "What's the best way to do that?"

"Just ask for Tim Diamond..."

"Just *use* Tim Diamond. He's sent us back here because he knows that our turning up again will panic the Mad American. He's already tried to kill us twice. He's certain to try again – and this time Moire will be watching. He's using us as bait in a trap, Tim. The Mad American kills us. Moire gets the Mad American. It's as simple as that."

I opened the guidebook. "I'm not sitting here, waiting to be shot," I said.

"Where do you want to be shot?" Tim asked.

"I don't want to be shot anywhere! That's why I'm going to find the Mad American before he finds us." I started to thumb through the pages. I still didn't know what I was looking for, but I had a good idea. "After we were knocked out, we were taken to the Mad American's headquarters," I said.

"But we were knocked out!" Tim said. "We didn't see anything."

"We didn't see much," I agreed. "But there were some clues. A blue star. Some words in a shop window – THE FRENCH CONFECTION. And when we were tied up, I heard something. Music. Singing."

"Do you think that was the Mad American?"

"No, Tim. It was coming from a building nearby." I stopped, trying to remember what I had heard. "It wasn't French singing," I said. "It was different… It was foreign."

Sitting next to me on the bed, Tim was making a strange noise. I thought for a moment that he had stomach-ache. Then I realized he was trying to hum the tune.

"That's right, Tim," I said. "It was something like that. Only a bit more human."

Tim stopped. I tried to think. How had the singing gone? It had been sad and somehow dislocated. A choir and a single male voice. At times it had been more like wailing than singing. Remembering it now made me think of a church. Was that it? Had it been religious music? But if so, what religion?

I'm not sure what happened first. The thought seemed to come into my mind at exactly the same moment as I found myself looking at the words *The Jewish Quarter* in the guidebook in my hands.

"Jewish music!" I exclaimed.

"Jewish?"

"The music that we heard, Tim. It was coming from a synagogue!"

Tim's eyes lit up. "You think we were taken to Jerusalem?"

"No, Tim. We were in Paris. But there's an area of Paris that's full of synagogues." I waved the book at him. "Le Marais. That's what it's called. The Jewish sector of Paris…"

"But how big is it?" Tim asked.

I read the page in front of me:

Originally a swamp, the Marais has grown to become one of the most fashionable areas of Paris. Its narrow streets are filled with shops and boutiques including some of the city's most elegant cafés and cake shops. The Marais is home to the Jewish quarter with numerous synagogues and kosher restaurants based around the Rue des Rosiers.

There was a map showing the area. It only had a couple of dozen roads. "It doesn't look too big," I said. "And at least we know what we're looking for. The French Confection."

"But what *is* The French Confection, Nick?"

"I think it must be a shop. Maybe it sells cakes or sweets or something. But once we've found it, we'll know we're right next to the factory. Find the sign and we'll have found the Mad American."

"And then?"

"Then we call Moire."

We slipped out of Le Chat Gris down the fire escape, dodging past Moire's men who were waiting for us at the front of the hotel. Then we dived into the nearest Metro station and headed north.

It was a short walk from the station to the start of Le Marais – the Place Vendôme, one of those Paris squares where even the trees manage to look expensive. From there we headed down towards a big, elegant building that turned out to be the Picasso museum. I'd studied Picasso at school. He's the guy who painted women with eyes in the sides of their necks and tables with legs going the wrong way. It's called surrealism. Maybe I should have taken Tim in, as he's pretty surreal himself. But we didn't have time.

We backtracked and found ourselves in a series of long, narrow streets with buildings rising five storeys on both sides. But I knew we were on the right track. There was no singing, but here and there I saw blue stars – the same stars I had glimpsed as I was bundled into the van. I knew what it was now: the six-pointed Star of David. There was one in every kosher food store and restaurant in the area.

We'd been following the Rue des Rosiers – the one I'd read about in the guidebook – but with no sign of the building where we'd been held. So now we started snaking up and down, taking the first on the right and the next on the left and so on. It was a pretty enough part of Paris, I'll say that for it. Tim had even forgotten our mission and stopped once or twice to take photographs. We'd been chased and threatened at knife-point. We'd been kidnapped, drugged and threatened again – this time by the French police. And he *still* thought we were on holiday!

And then, suddenly, we were there.

It was on one of the main streets of the area – the Rue de Sevigny. I recognized it at once: the burnt face of the building, the broken windows, the ugly chimney stacks... And there was the archway that we had driven through. There was a courtyard on the other side which was where the white van had been parked. I stood there in the sunlight, with people strolling past on the pavements, some carrying shopping bags, others pushing prams. And none of them knew. The biggest drug factory in Paris was right in front of them, just sitting there between a café and a cake shop, right in the middle of the Marais. I couldn't believe I had found it so easily. It was hard to believe it was there at all.

"Nick...!" Tim whispered.

I grabbed hold of him and pulled him down behind a parked car as Bastille and Lavache appeared, coming out of the front door and walking across the courtyard. Each of them had a heavy box in their hands. Another shipment on its way out! It made me angry that anyone should be dumb enough to want to buy drugs and angrier still that these two grim reapers would be getting richer by selling them.

"What do we do now?" Tim whispered.

"Now we call Moire," I said.

"Right!" Tim straightened up. "Let's ask in there!"

Before I could stop him he had walked across the pavement and into the cake shop. There was the sign in the window that I had seen from the van. THE FRENCH CONFECTION. Why did the name bother me? Why did I feel it was connected with something or someone I had seen? It was too late to worry about it now. Tim was already inside. I followed him in.

I found myself in a long, narrow shop with a counter running down one wall. Everywhere I looked there were cakes and croissants, bowls of coloured almonds and tiny pots of jam. The very air smelt of sugar and flour. On the counter stood one of the tallest wedding cakes I had ever seen: six platforms of swirly white icing with a marzipan bride and groom looking air-sick up on the top. There was a bead curtain at the back and now it rattled as the owner of the shop passed through, coming out to serve us. And of course I knew her. I'd met her on the train.

Erica Nice.

She stopped behind the counter, obviously as surprised to see us as we were to see her.

"You...!" she began.

"Mrs Nice!" Tim gurgled. I wondered how he had managed to remember her name. "We need to use your telephone. To call the police."

"I don't think so, Tim," I said.

Even as I spoke I was heading back towards the door. But I was already too late. Erica's hand came up and this time it wasn't holding an almond slice. It was the biggest gun I'd ever seen. Bigger than the wrinkled hand that held it. Its muzzle was as ugly as the smile on the old woman's face.

"But ... but ... but..." Tim stared.

"Erica Nice," I said. "I suppose I should have guessed. Madame Erica Nice. Say it fast and what do you get?"

"Madamericanice?" Tim suggested.

"Mad American," I said. "She's the one behind the drug racket, Tim. When we met her, she must have been checking the route. That's why she was on the train. And that's how Bastille and Lavache knew we were in Paris."

Erica Nice snarled at us. "Yes," she said. "I have to travel on the train now and then to keep an eye on things. Like that idiot steward – Marc Chabrol. He was scared. And scared people are no use to me."

"So you pushed him under a train," I said.

She shrugged. "I would have preferred to stab him. I did have my knitting needles, but unfortunately I was halfway through a woollen jumper. Pushing was easier."

"And what now?" I asked. I wondered if she was going to shoot us herself or call her two thugs to finish the job for her. At the same time,

I took a step forward, edging my way towards the counter and the giant wedding cake.

"Those idiots – Jacques and Luc – should have got rid of you when they had the chance," Erica hissed. "This time they will make no mistakes."

She turned to press a switch set in the wall. Presumably it connected the shop with the factory next door.

I leapt forward and threw my entire weight against the cake.

Erica half turned. The gun came up.

The door of the shop burst open, the glass smashing.

And as Erica Nice gave a single shrill scream and disappeared beneath about ten kilograms of wedding cake, Christien Moire and a dozen gendarmes hurled themselves into the shop. At the same time, I heard the blare of sirens as police cars swerved into the road from all directions.

I turned to Moire. "You followed us here?"

Moire nodded. "Of course. I had men on all sides of the hotel."

Erica Nice groaned and tried to fight her way out of several layers of sponge, jam and butter cream. Tim leaned forward and scooped up a fragment of white icing. He popped it into his mouth.

"Nice cake," he said.

THE WHITE CLIFFS

The next day, Christien Moire drove us up to Calais and personally escorted us onto the ferry. It would have been easier to have taken the train, of course. But somehow Tim and I had had enough of trains.

It had been a good week for Moire. Jacques Bastille and Luc Lavache had both been arrested. So had Erica Nice. The drug factory had been closed down and more arrests were expected. No wonder Moire wanted us out of the way. He was looking forward to promotion and maybe the Croix de Guerre or whatever medal French heroes get pinned to their right nipple. The last thing Moire needed was Tim and me hanging around to tell people the part we had played.

Moire stopped at the quay and handed us our tickets as well as a packed lunch for the crossing. "France is in your debt," he said, solemnly, and before either of us could stop him he had grabbed hold of Tim and planted a kiss on both cheeks.

Tim went bright red. "I know I cracked the case," he muttered. "But let's not get too friendly…"

"It's just the French way," I said. Even so, I made sure I shook hands with Moire. I didn't want him getting too close.

"I wish you a good journey, my friends," Moire said. "And this time, perhaps you will be careful what you say while you are on the ship!"

"We won't be saying anything," I promised. I'd bought Tim a Tintin book at the harbour bookstall. He could read that on the way home.

Moire smiled. *"Au revoir,"* he said.

"Where?" Tim asked. I'd have to translate it for him later.

We were about halfway home, this time chopping up and down on the Channel, when Tim suddenly looked up from the Tintin book. "You know," he said. "We never did find out how Erica Nice was smuggling the drugs on the train."

"Haven't you guessed?" I sighed and pulled out the blue sugar sachet that had started the whole thing. It was the sachet Tim had been given at the Gare du Nord. Somehow I'd never quite got round to opening it. I did so now.

There was a spoonful of white powder inside.

"Sugar?" Tim muttered.

"I don't think so, Tim," I replied. "This is just one sachet. But Erica Nice was transporting thousands of them every day on the train. A little parcel of drugs. One dose, already weighed and perfectly concealed." I tore open the packet and held it up. The powder was caught in the wind and snatched away. I watched it go, a brief flurry of white as it skimmed over the handrail and disappeared into the grey water of the English Channel.

"Do you think we ought to tell Moire?" Tim asked.

"I expect he's worked it out for himself," I said.

In the distance I could see the white cliffs of Dover looming up. We had only been away for a week but somehow it seemed a lot longer. I was glad to be home.

Tim was still holding the packed lunch that Moire had given us. Now he opened it. The first thing he took out was a strawberry yoghurt.

"Very funny," I said.

The yoghurt followed the drugs into the channel. Then we went downstairs to order fish and chips.

THE
BLURRED
MAN

THE PEN PAL

I knew the American was going to mean trouble, the moment he walked through the door. He only made it on the third attempt. It was eleven o'clock in the morning but clearly he'd been drinking since breakfast – and breakfast had probably come out of a bottle too. The smell of whisky was so strong it made my eyes water. Drunk at eleven o'clock! I didn't like to think what it was doing to him, but if I'd been his liver I'd have been applying for a transplant.

He managed to find a seat and slumped into it. The funny thing was, he was quite smartly dressed: a suit and a tie that looked expensive. I got the feeling straight away that this was someone with money. He was wearing gold-rimmed glasses, and as far as I could tell we were talking real gold. He was about forty years old, with hair that was just turning grey and

89

eyes that were just turning yellow. That must have been the whisky. He took out a cigarette and lit it. Blue smoke filled the room. This man would not have been a good advertisement for the National Health Service.

"My name is Carter," he said at last. He spoke with an American accent. "Joe Carter. I just got in from Chicago. And I've got a problem."

"I can see that," I muttered.

He glanced at me with one eye. The other eye looked somewhere over my shoulder. "Who are you?" he demanded.

"I'm Nick Diamond."

"I don't need a smart-arse kid. I'm looking for a private detective."

"That's him over there," I said, indicating the desk and my big brother, Tim.

"You want a coffee, Mr Carver?" Tim asked.

"It's not Carver. It's Carter. With a 't'," the American growled.

"I'm out of tea. How about a hot chocolate?"

"I don't want a hot anything!" Carter sucked on the cigarette. "I want help. I want to hire you. What do you charge?"

Tim stared. Although it was hard to believe, the American was offering him money. This was something that didn't happen often. Tim hadn't really made any money since he'd worked as a policeman, and even then the police dogs had earned more than him. At least they'd bitten the right man. As a private detective, Tim had been a total calamity. I'd helped him solve one or two cases, but most of the time I was stuck at school. Right now it was the week of half-term – six weeks before Christmas, and once again it didn't look like our stockings were going to be full. Unless you're talking holes. Tim had just seven pence left in his bank account. We'd written a begging letter to our mum and dad in Australia but were still saving up for the stamp.

I coughed and Tim jerked upright in his chair, trying to look businesslike. "You need a private detective?" he said. "Fine. That's me. But it'll cost you fifty pounds a day, plus expenses."

"You take traveller's cheques?"

"That depends on the traveller."

"I don't have cash."

"Traveller's cheques are fine," I said.

Joe Carter pulled out a bundle of blue traveller's cheques, then fumbled for a pen. For a moment I was worried that he'd be too drunk to sign them. But somehow he managed to scribble his name five times on the dotted lines, and slid the cheques across. "All right," he said. "That's five hundred dollars."

"Five hundred dollars!" Tim squeaked. The last time he'd had that much money in his hand he'd been playing Monopoly. "Five hundred dollars...?"

"About three hundred and fifty pounds," I told him.

Carter nodded. "Right. So now let me tell you where I'm coming from."

"I thought you were coming from Chicago," Tim said.

"I mean, let me tell you my problem. I got into England last Tuesday, a little less than a week ago. I'm staying in a hotel in the West End. The Ritz."

"You'd be crackers to stay anywhere else," Tim said.

"Yeah." Carter stubbed his cigarette out in the ashtray. Except we didn't have an ashtray. The smell of burning wood rose from the surface of Tim's desk. "I'm a writer, Mr Diamond. You may have read some of my books."

That was unlikely – unless he wrote children's books. Tim had recently started *Just William* for the fourth time.

"I'm pretty well-known in the States," Carter continued. "*The Big Bullet. Death in the Afternoon. Rivers of Blood*. Those are some of my titles."

"Romances?" Tim asked.

"No. They're crime novels. I'm successful. I make a ton of money out of my writing – but, you know, I believe in sharing it around.

I'm not married. I don't have kids. So I give it to charity. All sorts of charities. Mostly back home in the States, of course, but also in other parts of the world."

I wondered if he'd like to make a donation to the bankrupt brothers of dumb detectives, a little charity of my own. But I didn't say anything.

"Now, a couple of years back I heard of a charity operating here in England," he went on. "It was called Dream Time and I kind of liked the sound of it. Dream Time was there to help kids get more out of life. It bought computers and books and special equipment for schools. It also bought schools. It helped train kids who wanted to get into sport. Or who wanted to paint. Or who had never travelled." Carter glanced at me. "How old are you, son?" he asked.

"Fourteen," I said.

"I bet you make wishes sometimes."

"Yes. But unfortunately Tim is still here."

"Dream Time would help you. They make wishes come true." Carter reached into his pocket and took out a hip-flask. He unscrewed it and threw it back. It seemed to do him good. "A little Scotch," he explained.

"I thought you were American," Tim said.

"I gave Dream Time two million dollars of my money because I believed in them!" Carter exclaimed. "Most of all, I believed in the man

93

behind Dream Time. He was a saint. He was a lovely guy. His name was Lenny Smile."

I noticed that Carter was talking about Smile in the past tense. I was beginning to see the way this conversation might be going.

"What can I tell you about Lenny?" Carter went on. "Like me, he never married. He didn't have a big house or a fancy car or anything like that. In fact he lived in a small apartment in a part of London called Battersea. Dream Time had been his idea and he worked for it seven days a week, three hundred and sixty-five days a year. Lenny loved leap years because then he could work three hundred and sixty-six days a year. That was the sort of man he was. When I heard about him, I knew I had to support his work. So I gave him a quarter of a million dollars. And then another quarter. And so on…"

"So what's the problem, Mr Starter?" Tim asked. "You want your money back?"

"Hell, no! Let me explain. I loved this guy Lenny. I felt like I'd known him all my life. But recently, I decided we ought to meet."

"You'd never met him?"

"No. We were pen pals. We exchanged letters. Lots of letters – and e-mails. He used to write to me and I'd write back. That's how I got to know him. But I was busy with my work. And he was busy with his. We never met. We never even spoke. And then, recently,

I suddenly realized I needed a break. I'd been working so hard, I decided to come over to England and have a vacation."

"Wouldn't you have preferred a holiday?" Tim asked.

"I wrote to Lenny and told him I'd like to meet him. He was really pleased to hear from me. He said he wanted to show me all the work he'd been doing. All the children who'd benefited from the money I'd sent. I was really looking forward to the trip. He was going to meet me at Heathrow Airport."

"How would you know what he looked like if you'd never met?" I asked.

Carter blushed. "Well, I did sometimes wonder about that. So once I'd arranged to come I asked him to send me a photograph of himself."

He reached into his jacket and took out a photograph. He handed it to me.

The picture showed a man standing in front of a café in what could have been London or Paris. It was hard to be sure. I could see the words CAFÉ DEBUSSY written on the windows. But the man himself was harder to make out. Whoever had taken the photograph should have asked Dream Time for a new camera. It was completely out of focus. I could just make out a man in a black suit with a full-length coat. He was wearing gloves and a hat. But his face was a blur. He might have had dark hair.

I think he was smiling. There was a cat sitting on the pavement between his legs, and the cat was easier to make out than he was.

"It's not a very good picture," I said.

"I know." Carter took it back. "Lenny was a very shy person. He didn't even sign his letters. That's how shy he was. He told me that he didn't like going out very much. You see, there's something else you need to know about him. He was sick. He had this illness ... some kind of allergy."

"Was Algy his doctor?" Tim asked.

"No, no. An allergy. It meant he reacted to things. Peanuts, for example. They made him swell up. And he hated publicity. There have been a couple of stories about him in the newspapers, but he wouldn't give interviews and there were never any photographs. The Queen wanted to knight him, apparently, but sadly he was also allergic to queens. All that mattered to him was his work ... Dream Time ... helping kids. Anyway, meeting him was going to be the biggest moment of my life... I was as excited as a schoolboy."

As excited as a schoolboy? Obviously Carter had never visited my school.

"Only when I got to Heathrow, Lenny wasn't there. He wasn't in London either. I never got to meet him. And you know why?"

I knew why. But I waited for Lenny to tell me.

"Lenny was buried the day before I arrived," Carter said.

"Buried?" Tim exclaimed. "Why?"

"Because it was his funeral, Mr Diamond!" Carter lit another cigarette. "He was dead. And that's why I'm here. I want you to find out what happened."

"What did happen?" I asked.

"Well, like I told you, I arrived here at Heathrow last Tuesday. All I could think about was meeting Lenny Smile, shaking that man's hand and telling him just how much he meant to me. When he didn't show up, I didn't even check into my hotel. I went straight to the offices of Dream Time. And that was when they told me…"

"Who told you?" I asked.

"A man called Hoover. Rodney Hoover…"

"That name sucks," Tim said.

Carter ignored him. "He worked for Lenny, helping him run Dream Time. There's another assistant there too, called Fiona Lee. She's very posh. Upper-class, you know? They have an office just the other side of Battersea Bridge. It's right over the café you saw in that photo. Anyway, it seems that just a few days after I e-mailed Lenny to tell him I was coming, he got killed in a horrible accident, crossing the road."

"He fell down a manhole?" Tim asked.

"No, Mr Diamond. He got run over. Hoover

97

and Lee actually saw it happen. If they hadn't been there, the police wouldn't even have known it was Lenny."

"Why is that?"

"Because he was run over by a steamroller." Carter shuddered. Tim shivered. Even the desk light flickered. I had to admit, it was a pretty horrible way to go. "He was flattened," the American went on. "They told me that the ambulance people had to fold him before they could get him onto a stretcher. He was buried last week. At Brompton Cemetery, near Fulham."

Brompton. That was where the master criminal known as the Falcon had been buried too. Tim and I had gone to the cemetery at the end of our first ever case*. We were lucky we weren't still there.

"This guy Rodney Hoover tells me he's winding down Dream Time," Carter went on. "He says it wouldn't be the same without Lenny, and he doesn't have the heart to go on without him. I had a long talk with him in his office and I have to tell you … I didn't like it."

"You don't think it's a nice office?" Tim asked.

"I think something strange is going on."

Tim blinked. "What exactly do you think is strange?"

Carter almost choked on his cigarette. "Goddammit!" he yelled. "You don't think

* See *The Falcon's Malteser*

98

there's anything unusual in a guy getting run over by a steamroller? It happens in the middle of the night and just a few days before he's due to have a meeting with someone who's given him two million dollars! And the next thing you hear, the charity he'd set up is suddenly shutting down! You don't think that's all a little strange?"

"It's certainly strange that it happened in the middle of the night," Tim agreed. "Why wasn't he in bed?"

"I don't know why he wasn't in bed – but I'll tell you this: I think he was murdered. A man doesn't walk in front of a steamroller. But maybe he's pushed. Maybe this has got something to do with money … my money. Maybe somebody didn't want us to meet! I know that if I was writing this as a novel, that's the way it would turn out. Anyway, there are plenty of private detectives in London. If you're not interested, I can find someone who is. So are you going to look into this for me or not?"

Tim glanced at the traveller's cheques. He scooped them up. "Don't worry, Mr Carpark," he said. "I'll find the truth. The only question is – where do I find you?"

"I'm still at the Ritz," Carter said. "Ask for Room 8."

"I'll ask for you," Tim said. "But if you're out, I suppose the room-mate will have to do."

* * *

We changed the traveller's cheques into cash and blew some of it on the first decent meal we'd had in a week. Tim was in a good mood. He even let me have a pudding.

"I can't believe it!" he exclaimed, as the waitress served us two ice-cream sundaes. The service in the restaurant was so slow that they were more like Mondays by the time they arrived. "Three hundred and fifty pounds! That's more money than I've earned in a month."

"It's more money than you've earned in a year," I reminded him.

"And all because some crazy American thinks his pen pal was murdered."

"How do you know he wasn't?"

"Intuition." Tim tapped the side of his nose. "I can't explain it to you, kid. I've just got a feeling."

"You've also got ice-cream on your nose," I said.

After lunch we took the bus over to Fulham. I don't know why Tim decided to start in Brompton Cemetery. Maybe he wanted to visit it for old times' sake. It had been more than a year since we'd last been there, but the place hadn't changed. And why should it have? I doubted any of the residents had complained. None of them would have had the energy to redecorate. The gravestones were as weird as ever, some of them like Victorian telephone boxes, others like miniature castles with doors fastened by rusting chains and padlocks. You'd have needed a skeleton key to open them. The place was divided into separate areas: some old, some more modern. There must have been thousands of people there but of course none of them offered to show us the way to Smile's grave. We had to find it on our own.

It took us about an hour. It was on the edge of the cemetery, overshadowed by the football stadium next door. We might never have found it except that the grave had been recently dug. That was one clue. And there were fresh flowers. That was another. Smile had been given a lot of flowers. In fact, if he hadn't been dead he could have opened a florist's. I read the gravestone:

LENNY SMILE
APRIL 31st 1955 – NOVEMBER 11th 2001
A WONDERFUL MAN, CALLED TO REST.

We stood in silence for a moment. It seemed too bad that someone who had done so much for children all over the world hadn't even made it to fifty. I glanced at the biggest bunch of flowers on the grave. There was a card attached. It was signed in green ink, *With love, from Rodney Hoover and Fiona Lee.*

There was a movement on the other side

101

of the cemetery. I had thought we were alone when we arrived, but now I realized that there was a man, watching us. He was a long way away, standing behind one of the taller gravestones, but even at that distance I thought there was something familiar about him, and I found myself shivering without quite knowing why. He was wearing a full-length coat with gloves and a hat. I couldn't make out his face. From this distance, it was just a blur. And that was when I realized. I knew exactly where I'd seen him before. I started forward, running towards him. At that moment he turned round and hurried off, moving away from me.

"Nick!" Tim called out.

I ignored him and ran through the cemetery. There was a gravestone in the way and I jumped over it. Maybe that wasn't a respectful thing to do but I wasn't feeling exactly religious. I reached the main path and sprinted forward. I didn't know if Tim was following me or not. I didn't care.

The northern gates of the cemetery opened onto Old Brompton Road. I burst out and stood there, catching my breath. It came as a shock, coming from the land of the dead into that of the living, with buses and cabs roaring past. An old woman, wrapped in three cardigans, was selling flowers right next to the gate. Business can't have been good. Half the flowers were as dead as the people they were

102

meant for. I went over to her.

"Excuse me..." I said. "Did someone just come out through this gate?"

The old woman shook her head. "No, dear. I didn't see anyone."

"Are you sure? A man in a long coat. He was wearing a hat..."

"People don't come out of the cemetery," the old woman said. "When they get there, they stay there."

A moment later, Tim proved her wrong by appearing at the gate. "What is it, Nick?" he asked.

I looked up and down the pavement. There was nobody in sight. Had I imagined it? No. I was certain. The man I had seen in Joe Carter's photograph had been in the cemetery less than a minute ago. Once I'd spotted him, he had run away.

But that was impossible, wasn't it?

If it was Lenny Smile that I had just seen, then who was buried in the grave?

DEAD MAN'S FOOTSTEPS

We began our search for Lenny Smile the next day – at the Battersea offices of the charity he had created.

I knew the building, of course, from the photograph Carter had shown us. Dream Time's headquarters were above the Café Debussy, which was in the middle of a row of half-derelict shops a few minutes' walk from the River Thames. It was hard to believe that a charity worth millions of pounds could operate from such a small, shabby place. But maybe that was the point. Maybe they didn't want to spend the money they raised on plush offices in the West End. It's the same reason why Oxfam shops always look so run down. That way they can afford another ox.

But the inside of Dream Time was something else. The walls had been knocked through to create an open-plan area with carpets that reached up to your ankles and leather furniture you couldn't believe had started life as a cow. The light fittings looked Italian. Low lighting at high prices. There were framed pictures on the walls, of smiling children from around the world: Asia, Africa, Europe and so on. The receptionist was smiling too. We already knew that the place was being shut down, and I could see that she didn't have a lot to do. She'd just finished polishing her nails when we walked in. While we were waiting she started polishing her teeth.

At last a door opened and Fiona Lee walked in. At least, I guessed it must be her. We'd rung that morning and made an appointment. She was tall and slim, with her dark hair tied back in such a vicious bun that you'd expect it to explode at any moment. She had the looks of a model, but I'm talking the Airfix variety. All plastic. Her make-up was perfect. Her clothes were perfect. Everything about her was perfect, down to the last detail. Either she spent hours getting ready every morning, or she slept hanging in the wardrobe so that she didn't rumple her skin.

"Good morning," she said. Joe Carter had been right about her. She had such a posh accent that when she spoke you heard every letter. "My name is Fiona Lee."

We introduced ourselves.

She looked from Tim to me and back again.

She didn't seem impressed. "Do come in," she said. She spun round on her heel. With heels like hers I was surprised she didn't drill a hole in the floor.

We followed her down a corridor lined with more smiling kids. At the end was a door that led to an office on a corner, with views of Battersea Park one way and the Thames the other. Rodney Hoover was sitting behind a desk cluttered with papers and half-dead potted plants, talking on the telephone. An ugly desk for a very ugly man. Both of them looked like they were made of wood. He was running to fat and might have been a little less fat if he'd taken up running. He had drooping shoulders and jet black hair that oozed oil. He was wearing an old-fashioned suit that was too small for him and glasses that were too big. As he finished his call, I noticed that he had horrible teeth. In fact the last time I'd seen teeth like that, they'd been in a dog. Mrs Lee signalled and we sat down. Hoover hung up. He had been speaking with a strong accent that could have been Russian or German. I noticed he had bad breath. No wonder the potted plants on his desk were wilting.

"Good morning," he said.

"This is Tim Diamond, Mr Hoover," Mrs Lee said. She pronounced his name *Teem Daymond*. "He telephoned this morning."

"Oh yes. Yes!" Hoover turned to Tim. "I

am being sorry that I cannot help you, Mr Diamond." His English was terrible, although his breath was worse. "Right now, you see, Mrs Lee and I are closing down Dream Time, so if you have come about your little brother…"

"I don't need charity," I said.

"We helped a boy like you just a month ago," Fiona Lee said. She blinked, and her eyelashes seemed to wave goodbye. "He had always wanted to climb mountains, but he was afraid of heights."

"So did you buy him a small mountain?" Tim asked.

"No. We got him help from a psychiatrist. Then we paid for him to fly to Mount Everest. That little boy went all the way to the top! And although he unfortunately fell off, he was happy. That is the point of our work, Mr Diamond. We use the money that we raise to make children happy."

"And take the case of Billy!" Hoover added. He pointed at yet another photograph on the wall. If Dream Time had helped many more kids, they'd have run out of wall. "Billy was a boy who wanted to be a dancer. He was being bullied at school. So we hired some bullies to bully the bullies for Billy and now, you see, Billy is in the ballet!"

"Bully for Billy," I muttered.

"So how can we be of helping to you, Mr Diamond?" Hoover asked.

"I have some questions," Tim said. "About a friend of yours called Lenny Smile."

Both Rodney Hoover and Fiona Lee froze. Hoover licked his teeth, which can't have been a lot of fun. Fiona had gone pale. Even her make-up seemed to have lost some of its colour. "Why are you asking questions about Lenny?" she asked.

"Because that way people give me answers," Tim replied. "It's what I do. I'm a private detective."

There was an ugly silence. I had to say that it suited Rodney Hoover.

"Lenny is dead," he said. "You know very well that he's lying there in Brompton Cemetery. Yes? What could you possibly want to know about him?"

"I know he's dead," Tim said. "But I'd be interested to know exactly how he died. I understand you were there."

"We were there," Fiona said. A single tear had appeared in the corner of her eye and began to trickle down her cheek. "Poor, poor Lenny! It was the most ghastly, horrible moment in my life, Mr Diamond."

"I don't suppose it was a terrific moment for him either," I muttered.

She ignored me. "It was about eleven o'clock. Mr Hoover and myself had gone to see him. He didn't like to come out of his flat, so we often went round there to tell him how much money we had raised and how the charity was progressing. We talked. We had a glass of wine. And then we left."

"Lenny said he would come down with us to the car," Hoover continued. "It was a very beautiful night. He wanted to have some of the fresh air … you know? And so, we left the flat together."

"Lenny was a little bit ahead of us," Fiona Lee explained. "He was a fast walker. Mr Hoover stopped to tie his shoelaces and I waited for him. Lenny stepped into the road. And then…"

"The steamroller was going too fast." He swore quietly in a foreign language. Fiona sighed. "But the driver was on his way home. He was in the hurry. And he ran over Lenny!" He shook his head. "There was nothing, nothing we could do!"

"Do you know the driver's name?" Tim asked.

"I believe it is Krishner. Barry Krishner."

"Do you know what happened to him?"

"He is in a hospital for the hopelessly insane in north London … in Harrow," Fiona said. "You can imagine that it was a dreadful experience for him, running over a man with a steamroller. But it was his fault! And because he was speeding, he killed one of the most wonderful men who ever lived. Lenny Smile! I had worked for him for twenty years.

Mr Hoover too."

"You'd only worked for him for two years?" Tim asked.

"No. I worked with him also for twenty years," Hoover said. "But are you telling me, please, Mr Diamond. Who hired you to ask these questions about Lenny Smile?"

"I never reveal the names of my clients," Tim replied. "Joe Carter wants to remain anonymous."

"Carter!" Hoover muttered. He gave Tim an ugly look. It wasn't difficult. "I could have guessed this. Yes! He came here, asking all his questions as if Fiona and me..." He stopped himself. "There was not one thing suspicious about his death, Mr Diamond. It was an accident. We know. Why? Because we were there! You think someone killed him? Poppycock! Who would wish to kill him?"

"Maybe he had enemies," Tim said.

"Everybody loved Lenny," Fiona retorted. "Even his enemies loved him. All he did his whole life was give away money and help young people. That man built so many orphanages, we had to advertise for orphans to fill them."

"What else can you tell us about him?" I asked.

"It's hard to describe Lenny to someone who never met him."

"Try. Where did he live?"

"He rented a flat in Welles Road. Number seventeen. He didn't buy anywhere because he hated spending money on himself." She took out a tiny handkerchief and dabbed the corner of her eye. "It is true that he liked to be on his own a lot."

"Why?"

"Because of his allergies."

I remembered now. Carter had said he was sick.

"What was he allergic to?" I asked.

"Many, many things," Hoover replied. "Chocolate, peanuts, yoghurt, animals, elastic bands, insects…"

"If he was stung by a wasp, he would be in hospital for a week," Fiona agreed.

"He was also allergic to hospitals. He had to go to a private clinic." Hoover stood up. Suddenly the interview was over. "Lenny Smile was a very unique man. He was – as you say – one in a million. And you have no right … no right to come here like this. You are wrong! Wrong with all your suspiciousness."

"Yes." Fiona nodded in agreement. "His death was a terrible accident. But the police investigated. They found nothing. Mr Hoover and I were there and we saw nothing."

"You can say to your 'anonymous' client, Mr Carter, that he should go back to Chicago," Hoover concluded. "And now, please, I think you should leave."

We left. The last thing I saw was Rodney Hoover standing next to Fiona Lee. The two of them were holding hands. Were they just co-workers, friends … or something more? And there was something else. Hoover had said something. I wasn't sure what it was, but I was certain he had told me something that in fact he didn't want me to know. I tried to play back the conversation but it wouldn't come.

Tim and I left the offices of Dream Time together. Rodney Hoover and Fiona Lee had given us both the creeps. Neither of us said anything. But we both looked very carefully before we crossed the road.

At least Fiona had given us Smile's address, and as it wasn't far away that was where we went next.

Welles Road was round the back of Battersea, not far from the famous dogs' home. The tall, red-bricked buildings were all mansion flats … not as big as mansions, but certainly smarter than your average flat. There were a dozen people living in each block, with their names listed on the front door. It turned out that Smile had lived at 17A – on the fifth floor. We rang the bell, but there was no answer so we tried 17B. There was a pause, then a woman's voice crackled over the intercom.

"Who is it?"

"We're friends of Lenny Smile," I shouted

back before Tim could come up with a story of his own.

"The fifth floor!" the voice called out. There was a buzz and the door opened.

With its faded wallpaper and worn carpets, the building seemed somehow tired inside. And so were we by the time we got to the fifth floor. The lift wasn't working. The whole place smelled of damp and yesterday's cooking. I thought you needed to be rich to live in Battersea (unless, of course, you happened to be a dog). But anyone could have lived here if they weren't fussy. The fifth floor was also the top floor. The door of 17B was open when we arrived.

"Mr Smile is dead!"

The woman who had broken the news to us so discreetly was about eighty, with white hair that might have been a wig and a face that had long ago given up trying to look human. Her eyes, nose and mouth all seemed to have run into each other like a melting candle. Her voice was still crackling, even without the intercom system. She was dressed in a pale orange dress decorated with flowers; the sort of material that would have looked better on a chair. There were fluffy pink slippers on her feet. Her legs – what I could see of them – were stout and hairy and made me glad that I couldn't see more.

"Who are you?" Tim asked.

"My name's Lovely."

"I'm sure it is," Tim agreed. "But what is it?"

"I just told you, dear. Lovely! Rita Lovely! I live next door to Mr Smile. Or at least ... I used to."

"Have you moved?" Tim asked.

Mrs Lovely blinked at him. "No. Don't be daft! Mr Smile is the one who's moved. All the way to Brompton Cemetery!"

"We know that," Tim said. "We've already been there."

"Then what do you want?"

"We want to get into his flat."

"Why?"

I decided it was time to take over. "Mr Smile was my hero," I lied. I'd put on the little-boy-lost look that usually worked with very old women. And also, for that matter, with Tim. "He helped me."

"He gave you money?" She looked at me suspiciously.

"He saved my life. I had a rare disease."

"What disease?"

"It was so rare, it didn't have a name. Mr Smile paid for my medicine. I never got a chance to thank him. And I thought, if I could at least see where he lived..."

That softened her. "I've got a key," she said, taking it out of her pocket. "I was his neighbour for seven years and I used to look

114

after the place for him when he was away. You seem a nice boy, so I'll let you in, just for a few minutes. This way…"

It seemed to take her for ever to reach the door, but then she was very old. At last we were in. Mrs Lovely closed the door behind us and sat down to have a rest.

Smile's flat was small and ordinary. There was a living-room, but it was so neat and impersonal that it was hard to believe anyone had done any living there at all. There was a three-piece suite, a coffee table, a few ornaments. The pictures on the wall were even less interesting than the walls they hung on. It was the same story in the other rooms. The flat told us nothing about the person who had lived there. Even the fridge was empty.

"How often did you see Mr Smile?" I asked.

"I never saw him," Tim replied.

"I know, Tim. I'm asking Mrs Lovely."

"I hardly ever saw him," Mrs Lovely said. "He kept himself to himself, if you want the truth. Although I was here the night that he got run over."

"Did you see what happened?"

"Not really, no." She shook her head vigorously and then readjusted her hair and teeth. "But I did see him go out. There were two people with him, talking to him. They seemed to be helping him down the stairs."

"Helping him?"

"One on each side of him. A man and a woman…"

That would have been Rodney Hoover and Fiona Lee.

"After they'd gone, I heard the most terrible noise. It was a sort of rumble and then a scrunching. At first I thought it was my indigestion, but then I looked out of the window. And there they were! The two of them and the driver—"

"Barry Krishner…"

"I don't know his name, young man. But yes, the driver of the steamroller was there. He was looking as sick as a parrot. Hardly surprising!"

"What happened to the parrot?" Tim asked.

"There was no parrot!"

"You mean … it got so sick it died?"

"There was the driver, the two people I had seen on the stairs and blood all over the road!" Mrs Lovely sighed. "It was the worst thing I have ever seen, and I've lived through two world wars! Blood everywhere! Lots and lots and lots of blood…"

"Thank you," Tim interrupted, going pale.

"Were there no other witnesses?" I asked.

"Just one." Mrs Lovely leant forward. "There was a balloon-seller on the other side of the road. He must have seen everything. I've already been asked about him once, so before you ask me again let me tell you that

I don't know his name or where he had come from. He was an old man. He had a beard and about fifty helium balloons. Floating above his head."

"Why was his beard floating over his head?" Tim asked.

"The balloons, Tim!" I growled. I turned to Mrs Lovely. "Is there anything else you can tell us?" I asked. "Anything about Lenny Smile?"

"No. Not really." Suddenly there were tears in the old woman's eyes. She took out a handkerchief and blew her nose loudly. "I will miss him. It's true I hardly ever saw him, but he was a gentleman. Look at this note he sent me. It was my ninety-first birthday last week and he slipped it under the door."

She produced a crumpled sheet of paper, torn out of an exercise book. There were a couple of lines written in green ink:

Dear Mrs Lovely,
I hope you have a lovely birthday.
L.S.

That was all. The note couldn't have been less interesting or informative. And yet even so I thought there was something strange about it, something that didn't quite add up. I handed it back.

"Nobody else remembered my birthday," Mrs Lovely sighed. "I didn't get any cards. But then, most of my friends were blown up in the war…" She wiped her eyes. "I couldn't have asked for a more quiet neighbour," she said. "And now that he's gone, I'll really miss him."

How could she miss him when she had hardly ever met him? And why had Lenny Smile taken so much care not to be seen? I was beginning to realize that it wasn't just Carter's photograph that had been blurred. The same thing could be said for everything in Lenny Smile's life.

We found Barry Krishner, the steamroller driver, easily enough. There was only one institute for the hopelessly insane in Harrow. Well, two if you count the famous public school which was just a little further down the road. The hospital was a big, Victorian building, set in its own grounds with a path leading up to the front door.

"Are you sure this is the right place?" Tim asked.

"Yes," I said. "They've even got crazy paving."

I have to say, I was a bit worried about going into a mental asylum with Tim. I wondered if they'd let him out again. But it was too late to back out now. One of the doctors, a man called Eams, was waiting for us at the entrance. He was a short man, bald with a little beard that could have been bought at a joke shop. We introduced ourselves and he led us out of the winter sunlight into the gloomy heart of the building.

"Krishner has responded very well to treatment," he said. "Otherwise I would not let you speak with him. Even so, I must ask you to be extremely careful. As I am sure you can imagine, running someone over with a steamroller would be a very upsetting experience."

"For Lenny Smile?" Tim asked.

"For the driver! When Krishner first came here, he was in a state of shock. He ate very little. He barely spoke. Every night he woke up screaming."

"Bad dreams, Dr Eams?" Tim asked.

"Yes. But we have given him a lot of therapy and there has been considerable improvement. However, please, Mr Diamond, try not to refer to what happened. Don't mention any of the details – the steamroller, the accident itself. You have to be discreet!"

"Discreet is my middle name!" Tim nodded.

"And also please bear in mind, he is not a lunatic. He is here as my patient. So don't say anything that would make him think he is mentally ill."

Tim laughed. "I'd be mad to do that!" He nudged the doctor. "So, where's his padded cell?"

Barry Krishner was sitting in a small, old-fashioned room that could just as easily have belonged to a seaside hotel as an asylum. A large window looked out onto the garden and there were no bars. He was a small, grey-haired man, dressed in an old sports jacket and dark trousers. I noticed his eyes blinked a lot behind his spectacles, and he kept on picking his nails. Otherwise it would have been impossible to tell that he had, until recently, been in shock.

"Good afternoon, Barry," Dr Eams said. "These people want to ask you some very important questions about Lenny Smile." Krishner twitched as if he had just been electrocuted. Dr Eams smiled and continued in a soothing tone of voice. "You have nothing to worry about. They're not going to upset you." He nodded at Tim.

"It must have been a crushing experience," Tim began.

Krishner whimpered and twisted in his chair. Dr Eams frowned at Tim, then gently took hold of Krishner's arm. "Are you all right, Barry?" he asked. "Would you like me to get you a drink?"

"Good idea," Tim agreed. "Why not have a squash?"

Krishner shrieked. His glasses had slipped off his nose and one of his eyes had gone bloodshot.

"Mr Diamond!" Eams was angry now. "Please could you be careful what you say. You

120

told me you were going to ask Barry what he saw outside Lenny Smile's house."

"Flat," Tim corrected him.

Krishner went completely white. I thought he was going to pass out.

Dr Eams stared at Tim. "For heaven's sake…!" he rasped.

"OK, doc." Tim winked. "I think it's time we got to the crunch…"

Krishner began to foam at the mouth.

"I really want to crack this case. Although I have to say, the clues are a bit thin on the ground…"

Barry Krishner screamed and jumped out of the window. Without opening it. Alarms went off all over the hospital and, two minutes later, Tim and I were being escorted off the premises with the gates locked securely behind us.

"They weren't very helpful," Tim muttered. "Do you think it was something I said?"

I didn't answer. We had spent the whole day following in a supposedly dead man's footsteps. They had led us nowhere.

So where did we go now?

A NIGHT
AT THE CIRCUS

The next day was a Saturday. Tim was in a bad mood when he came in for breakfast. He'd obviously got out of bed the wrong side: not a good idea, since he slept next to the window. At least there was food in the fridge. The money that Joe Carter had paid us would last us a month, and that morning I'd cooked up eggs, bacon, tomatoes, sausages and beans. The papers had arrived – the *Sun* for me, the *Dandy* for Tim. An hour later the two of us were so full we could barely move. There's nothing like a great British breakfast for a great British heart attack.

But the truth is, we were both down in the dumps – and this time I don't mean the flat. We were no nearer to finding the truth about Smile. Rodney Hoover and Fiona Lee, the pair who ran Dream Time, were obviously creepy. According to Mrs Lovely, the next-door neighbour, they had half-carried Smile downstairs just before his fatal accident. Had he been drunk? Or drugged? They could have thrown him in front of the steamroller – but if so, why? As Tim would doubtless have said, they'd have needed a pressing reason.

Barry Krishner, the driver of the steamroller, hadn't been able to tell us anything. After his encounter with Tim, it would probably be years before he talked again. He might babble and jibber, but I guessed talking would be a little beyond him. The police had presumably investigated and found nothing. Maybe there was nothing to find.

And yet...

Part of me still wondered if Lenny Smile really was dead. I remembered the man I had glimpsed in Brompton Cemetery. He had looked remarkably like the man I had seen in the photograph, and had certainly taken off fast enough when I spotted him. But if Lenny wasn't dead, where was he? And who was it who had disappeared under the steamroller?

"I give up!" Tim exclaimed.

He seemed to be reading my mind. "This isn't an easy case," I agreed.

"No!" He pointed. "I'm talking about this crossword in the *Dandy!*"

I ignored him and flicked over the page in my newspaper. And that was when I saw it. It was on the same page as the horoscopes. An advertisement for a circus in Battersea Park.

Direct from Moscow
THE RUSSIAN STATE CIRCUS
Starring
The Flying Karamazov Brothers
Karl "On Your" Marx – The Human Cannon-ball
The Fabulous Tina Trotsky
Three Sisters on Unicycles
And much, much more!

There was a picture showing a big top, but it was what was in front that had caught my eye. It was a figure in silhouette. A man selling balloons.

"Look at this, Tim!" I exclaimed, sliding the newspaper towards him.

Tim quickly read the page. "That's amazing!" he said. "I'm going to meet an old friend!"

"What are you talking about?"

"My horoscope. That's what it says…"

"Not the horoscopes, Tim! Look at the advertisement underneath!"

Tim read it. "This is no time to be going to the circus, Nick," he said. "We're on a case!"

"But look at the balloon-seller!" I took a deep breath. "Don't you remember what Mrs Lovely said? There was a witness when Lenny Smile was killed. It was a man selling balloons. I thought that was odd at the time.

124

Why should there have been a balloon-seller in Battersea Park in the middle of the night?"

"He could have been lost…"

"I don't think so. I think he must have been part of the circus. There's a picture of him here in the paper. Maybe the balloon-seller was advertising the circus!"

"You mean … on his balloons?"

"Brilliant, Tim! Got it in one."

Tim ripped the page of the newspaper in half. He must have accidentally caught hold of the tablecloth, because he ripped that in half too. He folded the paper into his top pocket. "It's your turn to do the washing-up," he said. "Then let's go!"

In fact we didn't go back to Battersea until that evening. According to the advertisement, there was only one performance of the circus that day – at seven thirty – and I didn't see any point in turning up before. If the balloon-seller really was part of the big top, he'd probably be somewhere around during the performance. We would catch up with him then.

I don't know what you think about circuses. To be honest, I've never been a big fan. When you really think about it, is there anybody in the world less funny than a clown? And what can you say about somebody who has spent half their life learning how to balance thirty spinning plates and an umbrella on their nose?

OK. It's clever. But there simply have to be more useful things to do with your time! And, for that matter, with your nose. There was a time when they used to have animals – lions and elephants – performing in the ring. They were banned and I have to agree that was a good idea. But for my money they could ban the rest of the performers too, and put everyone out of their misery. I'm sorry. I've heard of people who have run away to join a circus, but speaking personally I'd run away to avoid seeing one.

But that said, I had to admit that the Russian State Circus looked interesting. It had parked its tent right in the middle of the park and there was something crazy and old-fashioned about the bright colours and the fluttering flags all edged silver by a perfect November moon. Four or five hundred people had turned out to see the show, and there were stilt-walkers and jugglers keeping the lines amused as they queued up to get in. As well as the tent itself there were about a dozen caravans parked on the grass, forming a miniature town. Some of these were modern and ugly. But there were also wooden caravans, painted red, blue and gold, that made me think of Russian gypsies and Russian palm-readers – old crones telling your future by candlelight. Tim had had his palm read once, when we were in Torquay. The palm-reader had laughed so much she'd had to lie down ... and that was only the contents of one finger on his left hand.

We bought tickets for the show. Tim wanted to see it, and having come all this way across London, I thought why not? We bought two of the last seats and followed the crowd in. Somehow the tent seemed even bigger inside than out. It was lit by flaming torches on striped, wooden poles. Grey smoke coiled in the air and dark shadows flickered across the ring. The whole place was bathed in a strange, red glow that seemed to transport us back to another century. The top of the tent was a tangle of ropes and wires, of rings and trapezes, all promises of things to come, but right now the ring was empty. There were wooden benches raked up in a steep bank, seven rows deep, forming a circle all round the sawdust. We were in the cheapest seats, one row from the back. As a treat, I'd bought Tim a stick of candyfloss. By the time the show started, he'd managed to get it all over himself as well as about half a dozen people on either side.

A band took its place on the far side of the ring. There were five players, dressed in old, shabby tailcoats. They had faces to match. The conductor looked about a hundred years old. I just hoped the music wouldn't get too exciting – I doubted his heart would stand it. With a trembling hand, he raised his baton and the band began to play. Unfortunately, the players all began at different times and what followed was a tremendous wailing and screeching as they all raced to get to the end first. But the conductor didn't seem to notice and the audience loved it. They'd come out for a good time and even when the violinist fell off his chair and the trombonist dropped his trombone they cheered and applauded.

By now I was almost looking forward to seeing the show … but as things turned out, we weren't going to see anything of the performance that night.

The band came to the end of its first piece and began its second – which could have been either a new piece or the same piece played again. It was hard to be sure. I was glancing at the audience when suddenly I froze. There was a man sitting in the front row, right next to the gap in the tent where the performers would come in. He was wearing a dark coat, a hat and gloves. He was too far away. Or maybe it was the poor light or the smoke. But once again his face was blurred. Even so, I knew him at once.

It was the man from the Brompton Cemetery. The man in the photograph at the Café Debussy.

Lenny Smile!

I grabbed hold of Tim. "Quick!" I exclaimed.

"What is it?" Tim jerked away, propelling the rest of his candyfloss off the end of his stick and into the lap of the woman behind him.

"There!" I pointed. But even as I searched for Lenny across the crowded circus, I saw him get up and slip out into the night. By the time Tim had followed my finger to the other side of the tent, he had gone.

"Is it a clown?" Tim asked.

"No, Tim! It's the blurred man!"

"Who?"

"Never mind. We've got to go…"

"But the circus hasn't even begun!"

I dragged Tim to his feet and we made our way to the end of the row and out of the big top. My mind was racing. I still didn't know who the man in the dark coat really was. But if it was the same person I had seen at the cemetery, what was he doing here? Could he perhaps have followed us? No – that was impossible. I was sure he hadn't seen us across the crowded auditorium. He was here for another reason, and somehow I knew it had nothing to do with spinning plates and custard pies.

We left the tent just as the ringmaster, a tall man in a bright red jacket and black top hat, arrived to introduce the show. I heard him bark out a few words in Russian, but by then Tim and I were in the open air with the moon high above us, the park eerie and empty and the caravans clustered together about thirty metres away.

"What is it?" Tim demanded. He had forgotten why we had come and was disappointed to be missing the show.

Quickly I told him what I had seen. "We've got to look for him!" I said.

"But we don't know where he is!"

"That's why we've got to look for him."

There seemed to be only one place he could have gone. We went over to the caravans, suddenly aware how cold and quiet it was out here, away from the crowds. The first caravan was empty. The second contained a dwarf sipping sadly at a bottle of vodka. As we made our way over to the third, a man dressed in a fake leopard skin walked past carrying a steel girder. Inside the tent I heard the ringmaster come to the end of a sentence and there was a round of applause. Either he had cracked a joke or the audience was just grateful he'd stopped talking. There was a drum roll. We approached the fourth caravan.

Lenny Smile – if that's who it was – had disappeared. But there was another dead man in Battersea Park that night.

I saw the balloons first and knew at once whose caravan this was. There were more than fifty of them, every colour imaginable, clinging together as if they were somehow alive and knew what had just happened. The strange thing was that they did almost seem to be cowering in the corner. They weren't touching the ground. But the balloon-seller was. He was stretched out on the carpet with something silver lying next to his outstretched hand.

"Don't touch it, Tim!" I warned.

Too late. Tim had already leaned over and picked it up.

It was a knife. The blade was about ten centimetres long. It matched, perfectly, the ten-centimetre deep wound in the back of the balloon-seller's head. There wasn't a lot of blood. The balloon-seller had been an old man. Killing him had been like attacking a scarecrow.

And then somebody screamed.

I spun round. There was a little girl there in a gold dress with sequins. She was sitting on a bicycle which had only one wheel, pedalling back and forth to stop herself falling over. She was pointing at Tim, her finger trembling, her eyes filled with horror, and suddenly I was aware of the other performers appearing, coming out of their caravans as if this was the morning and they'd just woken up. Only it was the middle of the night and these people weren't dressed for bed! There was a clown in striped pants with a bowler hat and (inevitably) a red nose. There was a man on stilts. A fat man with a crash helmet. Two more sisters on unicycles. The strong man had come back with his steel girder. A pair of identical twins stood like mirror images, identical expressions on their faces. And what they were all looking at

131

was my big brother Tim, holding a knife and hovering in the doorway of a man who had just been murdered.

The little girl who had started it screamed once more and shouted something out. The strong man spoke. Then the clown. It all came out as jibberish to me but it didn't take a lot of imagination to work out what they were saying.

"Boris the balloon man has been murdered!"

"Dear old Boris! Who did it?"

"It must have been the idiotic-looking Englishman holding the knife."

I don't know at what precise moment the mood turned nasty, but suddenly I realized that the people all around me no longer wanted to entertain us. The clown stepped forward and his face was twisted and ugly ... as well as being painted white with green diamonds over his eyes. He asked Tim something, his voice cracking with emotion and his make-up doing much the same.

"I don't speak Russian," Tim said.

"You kill Boris!"

So the balloon man really was called Boris. The clown was speaking English with an incredibly thick accent, struggling to make himself understood.

"Me?" Tim smiled and innocently raised a hand. Unfortunately it was the hand that was still holding the knife.

"Why you kill Boris?"

"Actually, I think you mean 'why *did* you kill Boris,'" Tim corrected him. "You've forgotten the verb..."

"I don't think they want an English lesson, Tim," I said.

Tim ignored me. "I kill Boris, you kill Boris, he killed Boris!" he explained to the increasingly puzzled clown.

"I didn't kill Boris!" I exclaimed.

"They killed Boris!" the clown said.

"That's right!" Tim smiled encouragingly.

"No, we didn't!" I yelled.

It was too late. The circus performers were getting closer by the second. I didn't like the way they were looking at us. And there were more of them now. Four muscle-bound brothers in white leotards had stepped out of the shadows. The ringmaster was staring at us from the edge of the tent. I wondered who was entertaining the audience. The entire circus seemed to have congregated outside.

The ringmaster snapped out a brief command in Russian.

"Let's go, Tim!" I said.

Tim dropped the knife and we turned and fled just as the performers started towards us. As far as they were concerned, Tim had just murdered one of their number, and this was a case of an eye for an eye – or a knife wound for a knife wound. These were travelling performers.

133

They had their own rules and to hell with the country in which they found themselves.

Tim and I took off across the park, trying to lose ourselves in the shadows. Not easy with a full moon that night. Something huge and solid sailed across the sky, then buried itself in the soft earth. The strong man had thrown his girder in our direction. We were lucky – he was strong, but he obviously had lousy aim. The girder would be found the next day sticking out of the grass like a bizarre, iron tree. Half a metre to the right and we'd have been found underneath it.

But I quickly realized that this was only the start of our troubles. The entire circus troupe had abandoned the performance in order to come after us. Word had quickly got round. We had killed old Boris and now they were going to kill us. There was a dull *whoomph!* and a figure shot through the air. It was the man in the crash helmet. This had to be Karl "On Your" Marx, the human cannon-ball. They had fired him in our direction, and I just had time to glimpse his outstretched fists as he soared through the night sky before I grabbed hold of Tim and threw him onto the grass. Marx whizzed past. We had been standing in front of an oak tree and there was a dull crunch as he hit the trunk, ending up wedged in a fork in the branches.

"Do you think he's OK?" Tim asked.

"I don't think he's oak anything!" I replied. "Come on!"

We scrabbled to our feet just as the clown set off across the grass, speeding towards us in a tiny, multicoloured car. I looked ahead with a sinking heart. We really were in the middle of nowhere, with grass all around, the river in the far distance and nobody else in sight. Anybody who had come to the park at that time of night would now be in the circus, watching the show.

"Run, Tim!" I gasped.

The clown was getting nearer. I could see his face, even less funny than usual, the grease paint livid in the moonlight. In seconds he would catch up with us and run us down. But then there was an explosion. The bonnet of the car blew open, the wheels fell off, water jetted off the radiator and smoke billowed out of the boot. The clown must have pressed the wrong button. Either that, or the car had done what it was designed for.

"Which way?" Tim panted.

I turned and looked back. For a brief, happy moment, I thought we had left the circus folk behind us, but then something whizzed through the darkness and slammed into the bark of another tree. It was a knife – but thrown from where? I looked up. There was a long telephone wire crossing the park, connected to a series of poles. And, impossibly, a man was standing,

135

ten metres above the ground, reaching for a second knife. It was a tightrope walker. He had followed us along the telephone wires and was there now, balancing effortlessly in mid-air. At the same time, I heard the sudden cough of an engine and saw a motorbike lurch across the lawn. It was being driven by one of the brothers in white leotards. He had two more brothers standing on his shoulders. The fourth brother was on top of the other two brothers, holding what looked horribly like an automatic machine-gun. The motorbike rumbled towards us, moving slowly because of the weight of the passengers. But as I watched, it was overtaken by the three sisters on their unicycles. The moonlight sparkled not only on their sequins but on the huge swords which one of the other performers must have given them. All three of them were yelling in high-pitched voices, and somehow I knew that I wasn't hearing a Russian folk song. The man on stilts came striding towards us, moving like some monstrous insect, throwing impossibly long shadows across the grass. Somehow he had got ahead of us. And finally, to my astonishment, there was a sudden bellow and a full-sized adult elephant came lumbering out of the trees with a girl in white feathers sitting astride its neck. This would have to be the lovely Tina Trotsky. And despite the law, the Russian State Circus did have an animal or two hidden in its big top.

They had an elephant! Did they also, I wondered, have lions?

Tim had seen it too. "They've got an elephant!" he exclaimed.

"I've seen it, Tim!"

"Is it African or Indian?"

"What?"

"I can never remember which is which!"

"What does it matter?" I almost screamed the words. "It won't make any difference when it stamps on us!"

The circus performers were closing in on us from all sides. There was a rattle from the machine-gun and bullets tore into the ground, ripping up the grass. The dwarf I had seen in the caravan had woken up. It now turned out he was a fire-eating dwarf ... at least, that might explain the flame-thrower he had strapped to his back. We had the elephant, the motorbike and the unicycles on one side. The dwarf and the stilt man were on the other. The tightrope walker was still somewhere overhead. The human cannon-ball was disentangling himself from the tree.

Things weren't looking good.

But then a car suddenly appeared, speeding across the grass. It raced past one of the unicyclists, knocking her out of the way, then curved round, snapping the stilt man's stilts in half. The stilt man yelled and dived head first into a bank of nettles. The elephant fell back, rearing up. Tina Trotsky somersaulted backwards, feathers fluttering all around her. The car skidded to a halt next to us and a door swung open.

"Get in!" someone said, and already I knew that I recognized the voice.

"Are you a taxi?" Tim asked. I think he was worrying about the fare.

"It doesn't matter what it is, Tim," I said. "Just get in!"

I pushed Tim ahead of me and dived onto the back seat. There was another rattle of machine-gun fire, a burst of flame and a loud thud as a second knife slammed into the side of the door. But then the car was moving, bouncing up and down along the grass. I saw a bush blocking the way, right in front of us. The driver went straight through it. There was a road on the other side. A van swerved to avoid us as our tyres hit concrete, and a bus swerved to avoid the van. I heard the screech of tyres and the even louder screech of the drivers. There was the sound of crumpling metal. A horn blared.

But then we were away, leaving Battersea Park far behind us.

It's like I said. I'd never liked the circus. And the events of the night had done nothing to change my mind.

THE REAL
LENNY SMILE

"Well, well, well. This is a very nasty surprise. The Diamond brothers! Having a night at the circus?"

It was the driver of the car, the man who had saved us, who was speaking. He had driven us directly to his office at New Scotland Yard. It had been a while since we had last seen Detective Chief Inspector Snape. But here he was, as large as life and much less enjoyable.

It had been Snape who had once employed Tim as a police-constable. He had been no more than an inspector then – and he'd probably had far fewer grey hairs. He was a big, solid man who obviously worked out in a gym. Nobody got born with muscles like his. He had small blue eyes and skin the colour of raw ham. He was wearing a made-to-measure suit but unfortunately it had been made to measure somebody else. It looked as if it was about to burst. His tie was crooked. So were his teeth. So were most of the people he met.

I had never known his name was Freddy but that was what was written on the door. He had an office on the fourth floor, overlooking the famous revolving sign. I had been involved with Snape twice before: once when we were on the trail of the Falcon, and once when he had forced me to share a cell with the master criminal, Johnny Powers*. He wasn't someone I'd been looking forward to meeting a third time – even if he had just rescued us from the murderous crowd at the Russian State Circus.

His assistant was with him. Detective Superintendent Boyle hadn't changed much since the last time I'd seen him either. *His* first name must have been "Push". That was what was written on his door. Short and fat with curly black hair, he'd have done well in one of those BBC documentaries about Neanderthal man. He was wearing a black leather jacket and faded jeans. As usual he had a couple of medallions buried in the forest of hair that sprouted up his chest and out of his open-necked shirt. Boyle looked more criminal than a criminal. He wasn't someone you'd want to meet on a dark night. He wasn't someone you'd want to meet at all.

"This is incredible!" Tim exclaimed. He turned to me. "You remember the horoscope

* See *Public Enemy Number Two*

140

in the newspaper! It said I was going to meet an old friend!"

"I'm not an old friend!" Snape exploded. "I hate you!"

"*I'd* like to get friendly with him," Boyle muttered. He took out a knuckleduster and slid it over his right fist. "Why don't you let the two of us go somewhere quiet, Chief...?"

"Forget it, Boyle!" Snape snapped. "And where did you get the knuckleduster? Have you been in the evidence room again?"

"It's mine!" Boyle protested.

"Well, put it away..."

Boyle slid the contraption off his hand and sulked.

Snape sat down behind his desk. Tim and I were sitting opposite him. We'd been waiting for him in the office for a couple of hours but he hadn't offered either of us so much as a cup of tea.

"What I want to know," he began, "is what the two of you were doing at the circus tonight. Why were the performers trying to kill you? And what happened to Boris the balloon-seller?"

"Someone killed him," I said.

"I know that, laddy. I've seen the body. Someone stuck a knife in him."

"Yeah." I nodded. "The circus people thought it was us."

"That's an easy enough mistake to make

141

when you two are involved." Snape smiled mirthlessly. "We went to the circus because we wanted to talk to the balloon-seller," he explained. "Luckily for you. But why were you interested in him? That's what I want to know."

"I wanted to buy a balloon," I said.

"Don't lie to me, Diamond! Not unless you want to spend a few minutes on your own with Boyle."

"Just one minute," Boyle pleaded. "Thirty seconds!"

"All right," I said. "We were interested in Lenny Smile."

"Ah!" Snape's eyes widened. Boyle looked disappointed. "Why?"

"We're working for a man called Joe Carter. He's American..."

"He thinks Lenny Smile was murdered," Tim said.

Snape nodded. "Of course Smile was murdered," he said. "And it was the best thing that ever happened to him. If I wasn't a police-man, I'd have been tempted to murder him myself."

Tim stared. "But he was a saint!" he burbled.

"He was a crook! Lenny Smile was the biggest crook in London! Boyle and I have been investigating him for months – and we'd have arrested him if he hadn't gone under that steamroller." Snape opened a drawer and took out a file as thick as a north London telephone directory. "This is the file on Lenny Smile," he said. "Where do you want me to begin?"

"How about at the beginning?" I suggested.

"All right. Lenny Smile set up a charity called Dream Time. He employed two assistants ... Rodney Hoover, who comes from the Ukraine. And Fiona Lee. She's from Sloane Square. We've investigated them, and as far as we can see they're in the clear. But Smile? He was a different matter. All the money passed through his bank account. He was in financial control. And half the money that went in, never came out."

"You mean ... he stole it?" I asked.

"Exactly. Millions of pounds that should have gone to poor children went into his own pocket. And when he did spend money on children, he got everything cheap. He provided hospitals with cheap X-ray machines that could only see halfway through. He provided schools with cheap books full of typing errrors. He took a bunch of children on a cheap adventure holiday."

"What's wrong with that?"

"It was in Afghanistan! Half the children still haven't come back! He bought headache pills that actually gave you a headache and food parcels where the parcels tasted better than the food. I'm telling you, Diamond, Lenny Smile was so crooked he makes an evening with Jack the Ripper sound like a nice idea! And I was this close to arresting him." Snape held his thumb and forefinger just millimetres apart. "I already had a full-time police officer watching his flat. It's like I say. We were just going to arrest him – but then he got killed."

"Suppose he isn't dead," I said.

Snape shook his head. "There were too many witnesses. Mrs Lovely, the woman who lived next door, saw him leave the flat. Hoover and Lee were with him. There was Barry Krishner, the driver. And Boris…"

"Wait a minute!" I interrupted. "Mrs Lovely didn't actually see anything. Barry Krishner has gone mad. I'm not sure Hoover and Lee can be trusted. And someone has just killed Boris." I remembered what Mrs Lovely had told us. "Mrs Lovely said that someone had been asking questions about the balloon-seller," I went on. "I thought she was talking about you … the police! But now I wonder if it wasn't someone else. The real killer, for example!" Snape stared at me. "I think Boris saw what really happened," I concluded. "And that was why he was killed."

"Who by?" Snape demanded.

"By Lenny Smile!"

There was a long silence. Snape looked doubtful. Boyle looked … well the same way Boyle always looks.

"What do you mean?" Snape demanded at length.

"It all makes sense. Lenny Smile knew that you were after him. You say you had a policeman watching his flat?"

Snape nodded. "Henderson. He's disappeared."

"Since when?"

"He vanished a week before the accident with the steamroller..."

"That was no accident!" I said. "Don't you get it, Snape? Smile knew he was cornered. You were closing in on him. And Joe Carter was coming over too. Carter wanted to know what had happened to all the millions he'd given Dream Time. So Smile had to disappear. He faked his own death, and right now he's somewhere in London. We've seen him! Twice!"

That made Snape sit up. "Where?"

"He was at the circus. He was in the crowd. We saw him about a minute before Boris was killed. And he was at the cemetery. Not underground – on top of it! I followed him and he ran away."

"How do you know it was Smile?" Snape asked.

"I don't. At least, I can't be sure. But I've seen a photograph of him and it looked the same."

"We don't know much about Smile," Snape

145

admitted. "Henderson was watching the flat, but he only saw him once. We know when he was born and when he died. But that's about all…"

"He didn't die. I'm telling you. Dig up the coffin and you'll probably find it's empty!"

Snape looked at Boyle, then back at me. Slowly, he nodded. "All right, laddy," he said. "Let's play it your way. But if you're wasting my time … it's your funeral!"

"There was no funeral," I said. "Lenny Smile isn't dead."

"Let's find out…"

I'll tell you now. There's one place you don't want to be at five past twelve on a black November night – and that's in a cemetery. The ground was so cold I could feel it all the way up to my knees, and every time I breathed the ice seemed to find its way into my skull. There were the four of us there – Snape, Boyle, Tim and myself – and now we'd been joined by another half-dozen police officers and workmen, two of whom were operating a mechanical digger that whined and groaned as it clawed at the frozen earth. Tim was whining and groaning too, as a matter of fact. I think he'd have preferred to have been in bed.

But maybe it wasn't just the weather that was managing to chill me. The whole thing was like a scene out of *Frankenstein*. You know the one – where Igor the deformed Hungarian servant has to climb into the grave and steal a human brain. Glancing at Boyle, I saw a distinct physical resemblance. I had to remind myself that two days ago I had been enjoying half-term and that the following day I would be back at school, with all the fun of double geography and French. In the meantime I had somehow stumbled into a horror film. I wondered what was going to turn up in the final reel.

The digger stabbed down. The earth shifted. Gradually the hole got deeper. There was a clunk – metal hitting wood – and two of the workmen climbed in to clear away the rest of the soil with spades. Snape moved forward.

I didn't watch as the coffin was opened. You have to remember that I was only fourteen years old, and if someone had made a film out of what was going on here I wouldn't even have been allowed to see it.

"Boyle!" Snape muttered the single word and the other man lowered himself into the hole. There was a pause. Then...

"Sir!"

Boyle was holding something. He passed it up to Snape. It was dark blue, shaped a bit like a bell, only paper thin. There was a silver disc squashed in the middle. It took me a few seconds to work out what it was. Then I realized. It was a police-constable's helmet.

But one that had been flattened.

"Henderson!" Snape muttered.

There had been a police-constable watching Smile's flat. He had disappeared a week before the accident. His name had been Henderson.

And now we knew what had happened to him.

"Don't you see, Tim? It was Henderson who was killed. Not Lenny Smile!"

The two of us were back at our Camden flat. After our hours spent in the cemetery, we were too cold to go to bed. I'd made us both hot chocolate and Tim was wearing two pairs of pyjamas and two dressing-gowns, with a hot-water bottle clasped to his chest.

"But who killed him?"

"Lenny Smile."

"But what about Hoover? And the woman? They were there when it happened."

For once, Tim was right. Rodney Hoover and Fiona Lee must have been part of it. Snape had already gone to arrest them. The man they had helped down the stairs must have been Henderson. I had been right about that. He had been drugged. They had taken him out of the flat and thrown him into the road, just as Barry Krishner turned the corner on his way home...

And yet it wasn't going to be easy to prove. There were no witnesses. And until Smile was found, it was hard to see exactly what he could do. Suddenly I realized how clever Smile had been. The blurred man? He had been more than that. He had run Dream Time, he had stolen all the money, and he had remained virtually invisible.

"Nobody knew him." I said.

"Who?"

"Smile. Mrs Lovely never spoke to him. Joe Carter only wrote to him. We went to his flat and it was like he'd never actually lived there. Even Rodney Hoover and Fiona Lee couldn't tell us much about him."

Tim nodded. I yawned. It was two o'clock, way past my bedtime. And in just five and a half hours I'd be getting ready for school. Monday was going to be a long day.

"You'll have to go to the Ritz tomorrow," I said.

"Why?"

"To tell Joe Carter about his so-called best friend."

Tim sighed. "It's not going to be easy," he said. "He had this big idea about Lenny Smile when all the time he was someone else!"

I finished my hot chocolate and stood up. Then, suddenly, it hit me. "What did you just say?" I asked.

"I've forgotten." Tim was so tired he was forgetting what he was saying even as he said it.

"Someone else! That's exactly the point! Of course!"

There had been so many clues. The note in the cemetery. Mrs Lovely and the card Lenny had sent her. The gravestone. The photograph of Smile outside the Café Debussy. And Snape...

"We know when he was born..."

But it was only now, when I was almost too tired to move, that it came together. The truth. All of it.

The following morning, I didn't go to school. Instead I made two telephone calls, and then later on, just after ten o'clock, Tim and I set out for the final showdown.

It was time to meet Lenny Smile.

THE BIG WHEEL

The tube from Camden Town to Waterloo is direct on the Northern line – which was probably just as well. I'd only had about five hours' sleep, and I was so tired that the whole world seemed to be shimmering and moving in slow motion. Tim was just as bad. He had a terrible nightmare in which he was lowered, still standing up, into Lenny's grave – and woke up screaming. I suppose it wasn't too surprising. He'd fallen asleep on the escalator.

But the two of us had livened up a little by the time we'd reached the other end. The weather had taken a turn for the worse. The rain was sheeting down, sucking any colour or warmth out of the city. We had left Waterloo station behind us, making for the South Bank, a stretch of London that has trouble looking beautiful even on the sunniest day. This is where you'll find the National Theatre and the National Film Theatre, both designed by architects with huge buckets of prefabricated cement. There weren't many people around. Just a few commuters struggling with umbrellas that the wind had turned inside out. Tim and I hurried forward without speaking. The rain lashed down, hit the concrete and bounced up again, wetting us twice.

I had made the telephone call just after breakfast.

"Mrs Lee?"

"Yes. Who is this?" Fiona Lee's clipped vowels had been instantly recognizable down the line.

"This is Nick Diamond. Remember me?"

A pause.

"I want to meet with Lenny Smile."

A longer pause. Then, *"That's not possible. Lenny Smile is dead."*

"You're lying. You know where he is. I want to see the three of you. Hoover, Lenny and you. Eleven o'clock at the London Eye. And if you don't want me to go to the police, you'd better not be late."

You've probably seen the London Eye, the huge Ferris wheel they put up outside County Hall. It's one of the big surprises of modern London. Unlike the Millennium Dome, it has actually been a success. It opened on time. It worked. It didn't fall over. At the end of the millennium year they decided to keep it, and suddenly it

152

was part of London – a brilliant silver circle at once huge and yet somehow fragile. Tim had taken me on it for my fourteenth birthday and we'd enjoyed the view so much we'd gone a second time. Well as they say, one good turn deserves another.

Not that we were going to see much today. The clouds were so low that the pods at the top almost seemed to disappear into them. You could see the Houses of Parliament on the other side of the river and, hazy in the distance, St Paul's. But that was about it. If there was a single day in the year when it wasn't worth paying ten pounds for the ride, this was it, which would explain why there were no crowds around when we approached: just Rodney Hoover and Fiona Lee, both of them wearing raincoats, waiting for us to arrive.

There was no sign of Lenny Smile, but I wasn't surprised. I had known he would never show up.

"Why are you calling us?" Hoover demanded. "First we have the police accusing us of terrible things. Then you, wanting to see Lenny. We don't know where Lenny is! As far as we know, he's dead..."

"Why don't we get out of the rain?" I suggested. "How about the wheel?" It seemed like a good idea. The rain was still bucketing down and there was nowhere else to go.

"After you, Mr Hoover..."

We bought tickets and climbed into the first compartment that came round. I wasn't surprised to find that there would only be the four of us in it for this turn of the wheel. The doors slid shut, and slowly – so slowly that we barely knew we were moving – we were carried up into the sky, into the driving rain.

There was a pause as if nobody knew quite what to say. Then Fiona broke the silence. "We already told that ghastly little policeman … Detective Chief Inspector Snape. Lenny was with us that day. He was killed by the steam-roller. And it is Lenny buried in the cemetery."

"No it isn't," I said. "Lenny Smile is right here now. He's on the big wheel. Inside this compartment."

"Is he?" Tim looked under the seat. "I don't see him!"

"That's because you're not looking in the right place, Tim," I said. "But that was the whole idea. You said it yourself last night. We all thought Lenny Smile was one thing, but in fact he was something else."

"You are not making the lot of sense," Hoover said. His face, already dark to begin with, had gone darker. He was watching me with nervous eyes.

"I should have known from the start that there was something strange about Lenny Smile," I said. "Nothing about him added up. Nobody – except you – had ever seen him. And

154

everything about him was a lie."

"You mean ... his name wasn't Lenny Smile?" Tim asked.

"Lenny Smile never existed, Tim!" I explained. "He was a fantasy. I should have known when I saw the details on the grave-stone. It said that he was born on 31st April 1955. But that was the first lie. There are only thirty days in April. 31st April doesn't exist!"

"It was a mistake..." Fiona muttered.

"Maybe. But then there was that photo-graph Carter showed us of 'Lenny' standing outside the Café Debussy. You told us that he was allergic to a lot of things, and one of those things was animals. But in the photograph there's a cat sitting between his feet – and he doesn't seem to care. The allergy business was a lie. But it was a clever one. It meant that he had a reason not to be seen. He had to stay indoors because he was ill..."

Centimetre by centimetre, the big wheel carried us further away from the ground. The rain was hammering against the glass. Looking out, I could barely see the buildings on the north bank of the river. There was Big Ben, but then the rain swept across it, turning it into a series of brown and white streaks.

Tim gaped. "So there was no Lenny Smile!" he exclaimed.

"That's right. Except when Hoover *pretended* to be Lenny Smile. Don't you see? He rented

155

the flat even though he never actually lived there. Occasionally he went in and out to make it look as if there was someone there. And of course it was Hoover who wrote that letter to Mrs Lovely."

"How do you know?"

"Because it was written in green ink. The message we saw in the card on Lenny's grave was also written in green ink – and it was the same handwriting. I should have seen from the start. It was Hoover we saw at the circus. And he was also there at Brompton Cemetery the day we visited the grave. I should have known it was him as soon as we met him at the Dream Time office."

"Why?" Tim asked.

"Because Hoover had never met us – but somehow he knew we'd been to Brompton Cemetery. Don't you remember what he said to us? 'You know very well that he's lying there in Brompton Cemetery.' Those were his exact words. But he only knew we knew because he knew who we were, and he knew who we were because he'd seen us!"

Tim scratched his head. "Could you say that last bit again?"

Fiona looked at me scornfully. "You're talking tommy-rot!" she said.

"Was Tommy part of this too?" Tim asked.

"Why would Rodney and I want to invent a man called Lenny Smile?" she continued,

156

ignoring him.

"Because the two of you were stealing millions of pounds from Dream Time. You knew that eventually the police would catch up with you. And there was always the danger that someone like Joe Carter would come over from America to find out what was happening to his money. You were the brains behind the charity. You were the 'big wheels', if you like. But you needed someone to take the blame and then disappear. That was Lenny Smile. Henderson – the policeman – must have found out what was going on, so he had to die too. And that was your brilliant idea. You'd turn Henderson into Lenny Smile. He went under the steam-roller and, as far as you were concerned, that was the end of the matter. Smile was dead. There was nothing left to investigate."

The pod was still moving up. There were a few pedestrians out on the South Bank. By now they were no more than dots.

"But now the police think Lenny Smile is alive," I went on. "That's why the two of you aren't in jail. They're looking for him. They don't have any proof against you. So the two of you are in the clear!"

Hoover had listened to all this in silence but now he smiled, his thin lips peeling back from his teeth. "You have it exactly right," he said. "Fiona and I are nobodies. We were just working for Lenny Smile. He is the real crook.

And, as you say, they have no proof. Nobody has any proof."

"Hoover dressed up as Lenny Smile…" Tim was still trying to work it all out.

"Only once. For the photograph that Joe Carter requested. But he was wearing the same coat and the same gloves when we saw him – which is why we thought he was Lenny Smile. Both times, he was too far away for us to see his face. And, of course, in the photograph the face was purposely blurred." I turned to Rodney. "I'd be interested to know, though. What were you doing in the cemetery?"

Hoover shrugged. "I realized that the bloody fool of an undertaker had made a mistake with the date on the gravestone. I went there to put it right. When I saw you and your brother at the grave, I knew something was wrong. I have to admit, I panicked. And ran."

"And the circus…?"

"Mrs Lovely told us there had been a witness. I had to track him down and make sure he didn't talk."

"But it wouldn't have mattered if he'd talked," Tim said. "He was Russian! Nobody would have understood."

"I don't believe in taking chances," Rodney said. His hand had slid into his coat pocket. Why wasn't I surprised, when it came out, to see that it was holding a gun?

"He's got a gun!" Tim squealed.

"That's right, Tim," I said.

"You've been very clever," Hoover snarled. "But you haven't quite thought it through." He glanced out of the window. We had reached the top of the circle, as high up as the Ferris wheel went. Suddenly Hoover fired. The glass door smashed. Tim leapt. The rain came rushing in. "An unfortunate accident!" Hoover shouted above the howl of the wind. "The door malfunctioned. Somehow it broke. You and your brother fell out."

"No we didn't!" Tim whimpered.

"Anyway, by the time they've finished wiping you off the South Bank, Fiona and I will have disappeared. The money is in a nice little bank in Brazil. We'll move there. A beach house in Rio de Janeiro! We'll live a life of luxury."

"That money was meant for sick children!" I shouted. "Don't you have any shame at all?"

"I cannot afford shame!" He gestured with the gun, pointing at the shattered glass and the swirling rain. "Now which one of you is going to step out first?"

"He is!" Tim pointed at me.

"No, I'm not," I said. I turned back to Hoover. "It won't work, Hoover. Why don't you take a look in the next pod?"

Hoover's eyes narrowed. Fiona Lee went over to the window. There were about twenty people in the pod above us on the London Eye.

All of them were dressed in blue. "It's full of policemen!" she exclaimed. She went over to the other side. "And the one below us! That's full of police too!"

"It must be their day out!" Tim said.

"Forget it, Tim." It was my turn to smile. "You've been set up, Hoover. Every word you've said has been recorded. The pod's bugged. Your confession is on tape right now, and as soon as the ride is over you and Fiona will have another ride. To jail!"

Fiona had begun to tremble. Hoover's eyes twitched. His grip tightened on the gun. "Maybe I'll kill you anyway," he said. "Just for the fun of it..."

And that was when the helicopter appeared – a dark-blue police helicopter, its blades beating at the rain outside the broken window. It had come swooping out of the clouds and now hovered just a few metres away. I could see Snape in the passenger seat. Boyle was in the back, dressed in a flak jacket, cradling an automatic rifle. I just hoped he was pointing it at Hoover, not at Tim.

"Why do you think the police released you?" I shouted above the noise of the helicopter. "I rang Snape this morning and told him what I'd worked out and he asked me to meet you. You walked into a trap. He knew you'd feel safe up in the air, just the four of us. He wanted you to confess."

A second later there was a crackle and Snape's voice came, amplified, from the helicopter. "Put the gun down, Hoover! The pod is surrounded!"

Hoover swore in Ukrainian, and before I could stop him he had twisted round and fired at the helicopter.

I threw myself at Hoover.

He fired a second time. But his aim had gone wild. The bullet hit Fiona in the shoulder. She screamed and fell to her knees.

Hoover, with my hands at his throat, crashed into the window. This one didn't break. I heard the toughened glass clunk against his un-toughened skull. His eyes glazed and he slid to the ground.

I turned to Tim. "Are you all right, Tim?" I asked.

"Yes, I'm fine." He pointed past the helicopter. "Look! You can see Trafalgar Square!"

It took another fifteen minutes for the pod to reach the ground. At once we were surrounded by uniformed police officers. Hoover and Lee were dragged out. They'd spend a few days in hospital on their way to jail. The helicopter with Snape and Boyle in was nowhere to be seen. With a bit of luck a strong gust of wind would have blown it out of London and maybe into Essex. The trouble with those two was that no matter how many times we helped them, they'd never thank us.

And I'd probably end up with a detention for missing a day of school.

"We'd better go to the Ritz," I said.

"For tea?" Tim asked.

"No, Tim. Joe Carter..."

The American was still waiting to hear about his best friend, Lenny Smile. I wasn't looking forward to breaking the bad news to him. Maybe I'd leave that to Tim. After all, discreet was his middle name.

It had stopped raining. Tim and I walked along the South Bank, leaving the London Eye behind us. There were workmen ahead of us, shovelling a rich, black ooze onto the surface of the road. On the pavement, a tramp stood with an upturned hat, playing some sort of plinky-plonk music on a strange instrument – a zither, I think. I found a pound coin and dropped it into the hat. Charity. That was how this had all begun.

"Ta!" the tramp said.

"Tar? Don't worry," Tim said. "I've seen it..."

We crossed the river, the sound of the zither fading into the distance behind.

I KNOW WHAT YOU DID LAST WEDNESDAY

AN INVITATION

I like horror stories – but not when they happen to me. If you've read my other adventures, you'll know that I've been smothered in concrete, thrown in jail with a dangerous lunatic, tied to a railway line, almost blown up, chased through a cornfield dodging machine-gun bullets, poisoned in Paris ... and all this before my fourteenth birthday. It's not fair. I do my homework. I clean my teeth twice a day. Why does everyone want to kill me?

But the worst thing that ever happened to me began on a hot morning in July. It was the first week of the summer holidays and there I was, as usual, stuck with my big brother Tim, the world's most unsuccessful private detective. Tim had just spent a month helping with security at the American Embassy in Grosvenor Square and even now I'm not sure how he'd decided that there was a bomb in the ambassador's car. Anyway, just as the ambassador was about to get in, Tim had grabbed hold of him and hurled him out of the way – which would have been heroic if there had been a bomb (there wasn't) and if Tim hadn't managed to throw the unfortunate man in front of a passing bus. The ambassador was now in hospital. And Tim was out of work.

So there we were at the breakfast table with Tim reading the morning post while I counted out the cornflakes. We were down to our last packet and it had to last us another week. That allowed us seventeen flakes each but as a treat I'd allowed Tim to keep the free toy. There was a handful of letters that morning and so far they'd all been bills.

"There's a letter from Mum," Tim said.

"Any money?"

"No..."

He quickly read the letter. It was strange to think that my mum and dad were still in Australia and that I would have been with them if I hadn't slipped off the plane and gone to stay with Tim. My dad was a door-to-door salesman, selling doors. He had a house in Sydney with three bedrooms and forty-seven doors. It had been two years now since I had seen him.

"Mum says you're welcome to visit," Tim said. "She says the door is always open."

"Which one?" I asked.

He picked up the last letter. I could see at

once that this wasn't a bill. It came in a square, white envelope made out of the sort of paper that only comes from the most expensive trees. The address was handwritten: a fountain-pen, not a biro. Tim weighed it in his hand. "I wonder what this is," he said.

"It's an envelope, Tim," I replied. "It's what letters come in."

"I mean … I wonder who it's from!" He smiled. "Maybe it's a thank-you letter from the American ambassador."

"Why should he thank you? You threw him under a bus!"

"Yes, but I sent him a bunch of grapes in hospital."

"Just open it, Tim," I said.

Tim grabbed hold of a knife, and – with a dramatic gesture – sliced open the mysterious envelope.

After we'd finished bandaging his left leg, we examined the contents. First, there was an invitation, printed in red ink on thick white card.

Dear Herbert, it began. Tim Diamond was, of course, only the name he called himself. His real name was Herbert Simple.

It has been many years since we met, but I would like to invite you to a reunion of old boys and girls from St Egbert's Comprehensive, which will take place from Wednesday 9th to Friday 11th July. I am sure you are busy

but I am so keen to see you again that I will pay you £1,000 to make the journey to Scotland. I also enclose a ticket for the train.
Your old friend,
Rory McDougal

Crocodile Island, Scotland

Tim tilted the envelope. Sure enough, a first-class train ticket slid out onto the table.

"That's fantastic!" Tim exclaimed. "A first-class ticket to Scotland." He examined the ticket. "And back again! That's even better!"

"Wait a minute," I said. "Who is Rory McDougal?" But even as I spoke, I thought the name was familiar.

"We were at school together, in the same class. Rory was brilliant. He came first in maths. He was so clever, he passed all his exams without even reading the questions. After he left school, he invented the pocket calculator – which was just as well, because he made so much money he needed a pocket calculator to count it."

"McDougal Industries." Now I knew where I'd heard the name. McDougal had been in the newspapers. The man was a multi-Mcmillionaire.

"When did you last see him?" I asked.

"It must have been on prize-giving day, about ten years ago," Tim said. "He went to

170

university, I joined the police."

Tim had only spent a year with the police but in that time the crime rate had doubled. He didn't often talk about it but I knew that he had once put together an identikit picture that had led to the arrest of the Archbishop of Canterbury. He'd been transferred to the mounted police but that had only lasted a few weeks before his horse resigned. Then he'd become a private detective – and of course, *he* had hardly made millions. If you added up all the money Tim had ever made and put it in a bank, the bank wouldn't even notice.

"Are you going?" I asked.

Tim flicked a cornflake towards his mouth. It disappeared over his shoulder. "Of course I'm going," he said. "Maybe McNoodle will offer me a job. Head of Security on Alligator Island."

"Crocodile Island, Tim." I picked up the invitation. "What about me?"

"Sorry, kid. I didn't see your name on the envelope."

"Maybe it's under the stamp." Tim said nothing, so I went on, "You can't leave me here."

"Why not?"

"I'm only fourteen. It's against the law."

Tim frowned. "I won't tell if you won't tell."

"I will tell."

"Forget it, Nick. McStrudel is my old

schoolfriend. He went to my old school. It's my name on the envelope and you can argue all you like. But this time, I'm going alone."

We left King's Cross station on the morning of the 9th.

Tim sat next to the window, looking sulky. I was sitting opposite him. I had finally persuaded him to swap the first-class ticket for two second-class ones, which at least allowed me to travel free. You may think it strange that I should have wanted to join Tim on a journey heading several hundred miles north. But there was something about the invitation that bothered me. Maybe it was the letter, written in ink the colour of blood. Maybe it was the name – Crocodile Island. And then there was the money. The invitation might have sounded innocent enough, but why was McDougal paying Tim £1,000 to get on the train? I had a feeling that there might be more to this than a school reunion. And for that matter, why would anyone in their right mind want to be reunited with Tim?

I was also curious. It's not every day that you get to meet a man like Rory McDougal. Computers, camcorders, mobile phones and DVD players ... they all came stamped with the initials RM. And every machine that sold made McDougal a little richer.

Apparently the man was something of a

172

recluse. A few years back he'd bought himself an island off the Scottish coast, somewhere to be alone. There had been pictures of it in all the newspapers. The island was long and narrow with two arms jutting out and a twisting tail. Apparently, that was how it had got its name.

Tim didn't say much on the journey. To cheer him up, I'd bought him a *Beano* comic and perhaps he was having trouble with the long words. It took us about four hours to get to Scotland and it took another hour before I noticed. There were no signs, no frontier post, no man in a kilt playing the bagpipes and munching haggis as the train went past. It was only when the ticket collector asked us for our tickets and Tim couldn't understand a word he was saying that I knew we must be close. Sure enough, a few minutes later the train slowed down and Tim got out. Personally, I would have waited until the train had actually stopped, but I suppose he was over-excited.

Fortunately he was only bruised and we managed the short walk down to the harbour where an old fishing boat was waiting for us. The boat was called the *Silver Medal* and a small crowd of people were waiting to go on board.

"My God!" one of them exclaimed. "It's Herbert Simple! I never thought I'd see *him* again!"

The man who had spoken was fat and bald, dressed in a three-piece suit. If he ate much more, it would soon be a four-piece suit. His trousers were already showing the strain. His name, it turned out, was Eric Draper. He was a lawyer.

Tim smiled. "I changed my name," he announced. "It's Tim Diamond now."

They all had a good laugh at that.

"And who is he?" Eric asked. I suddenly realized he was looking at me.

"That's my kid brother, Nick."

"So what are you doing now ... Tim?" one of the women asked in a high-pitched voice. She had glasses and long, curly hair and such large teeth that she seemed to have trouble closing her mouth. Her name was Janet Rhodes.

Tim put on his "don't mess with me" face. Unfortunately, it just made him look seasick. "Actually," he drawled, "I'm a private detective."

"Really?" Eric roared with laughter. His suit shuddered and one of the buttons flew off. "I can't believe Rory invited you here too. As I recall, you were the stupidest boy at St Egbert's. I still remember your performance as Hamlet in the school play."

"What was so stupid about that?" I asked.

"Nothing. Except everyone else was doing Macbeth."

One of the other women stepped forward.

She was small and drab-looking, dressed in a mousy coat that had seen better days. She was eating a chocolate flake. "Hello … Tim!" she said shyly. "I bet you don't remember me!"

"Of course I remember you!" Tim exclaimed. "You're Lisa Beach!"

"No I'm not! I'm Sylvie Binns." She looked disappointed. "You gave me my first kiss behind the bike shed. Don't you remember?"

Tim frowned. "I remember the bike shed…" he said.

There was a loud blast from the boat and the captain appeared, looking over the side. He had one leg, one eye and a huge beard. All that was missing was the parrot and he could have got a job in any pantomime in town. "All aboard!" he shouted. "Departing for Crocodile Island!"

We made our way up the gangplank. The boat was old and smelly. So was the captain. The eight of us stood on the deck while he pulled up the anchor, and a few minutes later we were off, the engine rattling as if it was about to fall out of the boat. It occurred to me that the Silver Medal was a strange choice of boat for a multi-millionaire. What had happened to the deluxe yacht? But nobody else had noticed, so I said nothing.

Apart from Eric, Janet and Sylvie, there were three other people on board: two more women and another man, a fit-looking black guy dressed in jeans and a sweatshirt.

"That's Mark Tyler," Tim told me as we cut through the waves, leaving the mainland behind us. "He came first at sport at St Egbert's..."

I knew the name. Tyler had been in the British Olympic athletics team at Atlanta.

"He used to run to school and run home again," Tim went on. "He was so fast, he used to overtake the school bus. When he went cross-country running, he actually left the country, which certainly made the headmaster very cross. He's a brilliant sportsman!"

That just left the two other women.

Brenda Blake was an opera singer and looked it. Big and muscular, she had the sort of arms you'd expect to find on a Japanese wrestler – or perhaps around his belly.

Libby Goldman was big and blonde and worked in children's TV, presenting a television programme called *Libby's Lounge*. She sang, danced, juggled and did magic tricks ... and all this before we'd even left the quay. It was a shame that in real life we couldn't turn her off.

The journey took about an hour, by which time the coast of Scotland had become just a grey smudge behind us. Slowly Crocodile Island sneaked up on us. It was about half a mile long, rising to a point at what must have been its "tail", with sheer cliffs sweeping down into the sea. There were six jagged pillars of rock at this end, making a landing impossible. But at the other end, in the shelter of the crocodile's arm, someone had built a jetty. As the boat drew in, I noticed a security camera watching us from above.

"Here we are, ladies and gentlemen," the captain announced from somewhere behind his beard. "I wish you all a very pleasant stay on Crocodile Island. I do indeed! I'll be coming back for you in a couple of days. My name is Captain Randle, by the way. Horatio Randle. It's been a pleasure having you lovely people on my boat. You remember me, now!"

"Aren't you coming with us?" Eric demanded.

"No, sir. I'm not invited," Captain Randle replied. "I live on the mainland. But I'll be back to collect you in a couple of days. I'll see you then!"

We disembarked. The boat pulled out and headed back the way it had come. The eight of us were left on the island, wondering what was going to happen next.

"So where's old Rory?" Brenda asked.

"Maybe we should walk up to the house," Sylvie suggested. She was the only one of them who didn't have a full-time job. She had told Tim that she was a housewife, and was carrying three photographs of her husband and three more of her house.

"Bit of a cheek," Eric muttered. From the look of him, walking wasn't something he did often.

"Best foot forward!" Janet said cheerily. Apparently she worked as a hairdresser, and her own hair was dancing in the wind. As indeed was Libby.

We walked. Sylvie might have called it a house but I would have said it was a castle that Rory had bought for himself on his island retreat. It was built out of grey brick: a grand, sprawling building with towers and battlements and even gargoyles gazing wickedly out of the corners. We reached the front door. It was solid oak, as thick as a tree and half as welcoming.

"I wonder if we should knock?" Tim asked.

"To hell with that!" Eric pushed and the door swung open.

We found ourselves in a great hall with a black and white floor, animal heads on the walls and a roaring fire in the hearth. A grand-father clock chimed four times. I looked at my watch – it was actually ten past three. I was already beginning to feel uneasy. Apart from the crackle of the logs and the ticking of the clock, the house was silent. It felt empty. No Rory, no Mrs Rory, no butler, no cook. Just us.

"Hello?" Libby called out. "Is there anyone at home?"

"It-doesn't-look-as-if-there's-anyone-here,"

178

Mark said. At least, I think that's what he said. Speaking was something else that he did very fast. Whole sentences came out of his mouth as a single word.

"This is ridiculous," Eric snapped. "I suggest we split up and try and find Rory. Maybe he's asleep upstairs."

So we all went our separate ways. Mark and Eric headed off through different doors. Libby Goldman went into the kitchen. Tim and I went upstairs. It was only now that we were inside it that I realized just how big this house was. It had five staircases, doors everywhere and so many corridors that we could have been walking through a maze. And if it looked like a castle from the outside, inside it was like a museum. There was more furniture than you'd find in a department store. Antique chairs and sofas stood next to cupboards and sideboards and tables of every shape and size. There were so many oil paintings that you could hardly see the walls. Rory also seemed to have a fondness for ancient weapons – I had only been in the place a few minutes but already I had seen crossbows and muskets and flintlock pistols mounted on wooden plaques. On the first floor there was a stuffed bear holding an Elizabethan gun ... a blunderbuss. The stairs and upper landing were covered in thick, red carpet which muffled every sound. In the distance I could hear Janet calling out Rory's name but it was difficult to say if she was near or far away. Suddenly we were lost and very much on our own.

We reached a corner where there was a suit of dull silver armour standing guard; a knight with a shield but no sword.

"I don't like it," I said.

"I think it's a very nice suit of armour," Tim replied.

"I'm not talking about the armour, Tim," I said. "I'm talking about the whole island. Why isn't there anyone here to meet us? And why did your friend send that old fishing boat to pick us up?"

Tim smiled. "Relax, kid," he said. "The house is a bit quiet, that's all. But my sixth sense would tell me if there was something wrong, and right now I'm feeling fine…"

Just then there was a high-pitched scream from another part of the second floor. It was Brenda. She screamed and screamed again.

"How lovely!" Tim exclaimed. "Brenda's singing for us! I think that's Mozart, isn't it?"

"It's not Mozart, Tim," I shouted, beginning to run towards the sound. "She's screaming for help! Come on!"

We ran down the corridor and round the corner. That was when we saw Brenda, standing in front of an open bedroom door. She had stopped screaming now but her face was white and her hands were tearing at her hair. At the same time, Libby and Sylvie appeared, coming up the stairs. And Eric was also there, pushing his way forward to see what the fuss was about.

Tim and I reached the doorway. I looked inside.

The room had a red carpet. It took me a couple of seconds to realize that the room had once had a yellow carpet. It was covered in blood. There was more blood on the walls and on the bed. There was even blood on the blood.

And there was McDougal. I'm afraid it was the end of the story for Rory. The sword that had killed him was lying next to him and I guess it must have been taken from the suit of armour.

Brenda screamed again and pulled out a handful of her own hair.

Eric stood back, gasping.

Libby burst into tears.

And Tim, of course, fainted.

There were just the eight of us, trapped on Crocodile Island. And I had to admit, our reunion hadn't got off to a very good start.

AFTER DARK

"It was horrible," Tim groaned. "It was horrible. Rory McPoodle ... he was in pieces!"

"I don't want to hear about it, Tim," I said. Actually, it was too late. He'd already told me twenty times.

"Why would anyone *do* that?" he demanded. "What sort of person would do that?"

"I'm not sure," I muttered. "How about a dangerous lunatic?"

Tim nodded. "You could be right," he said.

We were sitting in our bedroom. We knew it was the bedroom that McDougal had prepared for us because it had Tim's name on the door. There were seven bedrooms on the same floor, each one of them labelled for the arriving guests. This room was square, with a high ceiling and a window with a low balcony looking out over a sea that was already grey and choppy as the sun set and the evening drew in.

There was a four-poster bed, a heavy tapestry and the sort of wallpaper that could give you bad dreams. There was also something else I'd noticed and it worried me.

"Look at this, Tim," I said. I pointed at the bedside table. "There's a telephone socket here – but no telephone. What does that tell you?"

"The last person who slept in this room stole the telephone?"

"Not exactly. I think the telephone has been taken to stop us making any calls."

"Why would anyone do that?"

"To stop us reporting the death of Rory McDougal to the police."

Tim considered. "You mean … someone knew we were coming…" he began.

"Exactly. And they also knew we'd be stuck here. At least until the boat came back."

It was a nasty thought. I was beginning to have lots of nasty thoughts, and the worst one was this: someone had killed Rory McDougal, but had it happened before we arrived on the island? Or had he been killed by one of the people from the boat? As soon as we had arrived at the house, we had all split up. For at least ten minutes nobody had known where anybody else was, which meant that any one of us could have found Rory and killed him before the others arrived.

Along with Tim and myself, there were now six people on the island … six and several halves if you counted Rory. Eric Draper, Janet Rhodes, Sylvie Binns, Mark Tyler, Brenda Blake and Libby Goldman. Tim hadn't seen any of them in ten years and knew hardly anything about them. Could one of them be a crazed killer? Could one of them have planned this whole thing?

I looked at my watch. It was ten to seven. We left the room and went back downstairs.

Eric Draper had called a meeting in the dining-room at seven o'clock. I don't know who had put him in charge but I guessed he had decided himself.

"He was head boy at school," Tim told me. "He was always telling everyone what to do. Even the teachers used to do what he said."

"What was Rory McDougal like as a boy?"

"Well ... he was young."

"That's very helpful, Tim. I mean ... was he popular?"

"Yes. Except he once had a big row with Libby Goldman. He tried to kiss her in biology class and she attacked him with a bicycle pump."

"But she wouldn't kill him just because of that, would she?"

"You should have seen where she put the bicycle pump!"

In fact Libby was alone in the dining-room when we arrived for the meeting. She was sitting in a chair at the end of a black, polished

184

table that ran almost the full length of the room. Portraits of bearded men in different shades of tartan looked down from the walls. A chandelier hung from the ceiling.

She looked up as we came in. Her eyes were red. Either she had been crying or she had bad hay fever – and I hadn't noticed any hay on Crocodile Island. She was smoking a cigarette – or trying to. Her hands were shaking so much she had trouble getting it into her mouth.

"What are we going to do?" she wailed. "It's so horrible! I knew I shouldn't have accepted Rory's invitation!"

"Why did you?" I asked. "If you didn't like him…"

"Well … he's interesting. He's rich. I thought he might appear on my television programme – Libby's Lounge."

"I watch that!" Tim exclaimed.

"But it's a children's programme," Libby said.

Tim blushed. "Well … I mean … I've seen it. A bit of it."

"I've never heard of it," I muttered.

Libby's eyes went redder.

Then three of the others came in: Janet Rhodes, Mark Tyler and Brenda Blake.

"I've been trying to call the mainland on my mobile phone," Janet announced. "But I can't get a signal."

"I can't get a signal either," agreed Mark,

speaking as quickly as ever. He sort of shim-mered in front of me and suddenly he was sitting down.

"There is no signal on this island."

"And no phone in my room," Janet said.

"No phone in any room!" The singer was looking pale and scared. Of course, she was the one who had found the body. Looking at her, I saw that it would be a few months before she sang in a concert hall. She probably wouldn't have the strength to sing in the bath.

Somewhere a clock struck seven and Eric Draper waddled into the room. "Are we all here?" he asked.

"I'm here!" Tim called out, as helpful as ever.

"I think there's one missing," I said.

Eric Draper did a quick head count. At least everyone in the room still had their heads. "Sylvie isn't here yet," he said. He scowled. You could tell he was the sort of man who expected everyone to do exactly what he said. "We'll have to wait for her."

"She was always late for everything," Janet muttered. She had slumped into a chair next to Libby. "I don't know how she managed to come first in chemistry. She was always late for class."

"I saw her in her room a few moments ago," Mark said. "She was sitting on the bed. She looked upset."

"I'm upset!" Eric said. "We're all upset!

Well, let's begin without her." He cleared his throat as if we were the jury and he was about to begin his summing up. "We are clearly in a very awkward situation here. We've been invited to this island, only to discover that our host, Rory McDougal, has been murdered. We can't call the police because it would seem that there are no telephones and none of our mobiles can get a signal. Unless we can find a boat to get back to the mainland, we're stuck here until Captain Randle – or whatever his name was – arrives to pick us up. The only good news is that there's plenty of food in the house. I've looked in the kitchen. This is a comfortable house. We should be fine here."

"Unless the killer strikes again," I said.

Everyone looked at me. "What makes you think he'll do that?" Eric demanded.

"It's a possibility," I said. "And anyway, 'he' could be a 'she'."

I noticed Libby shivered when I said that – but to be frank she'd been shivering a lot recently.

"Did Rory invite you here too?" Mark asked.

"Not exactly. He invited Tim, and Tim couldn't leave me on my own at home. So I came along for the ride."

Eric scowled for a second time. Scowling suited him. "I wouldn't have said this place was suitable for children," he said.

"Murder isn't suitable for children," I agreed. "But I'm stuck here with you and it seems to me that we've all been set up. No phones! That has to be on purpose. All the rooms were prepared for us, with our names on the doors. And now, like you say, we're stuck here. Suppose the killer is here too?"

"That's not possible," Brenda whispered. But she didn't sound like she believed herself.

"Maybe Rory wasn't murdered," Tim suggested. "Maybe it was an accident."

"You mean someone accidentally chopped him to pieces?" I asked.

Janet glanced at the door. She was looking nervous. A hairdresser having a bad hair day. "Perhaps we should go and find Sylvie," she suggested.

Nobody said anything. Then, as one, we hurried out of the room.

We went back upstairs. Sylvie's room was halfway down the corridor, two doors away from our own. It was closed. Tim knocked. There was no reply. "She could have fallen asleep," he said.

"Just open the door, Tim," I suggested.

He opened it. Sylvie's room was a similar size to ours but with more modern furniture, an abstract painting on the wall and two single beds. Her case was standing beside the wall, unopened. As my eyes travelled towards her, I noticed a twist of something silver lying in the

188

middle of the yellow carpet. But I didn't have time to mention it.

Sylvie was lying on her back, one hand flung out. When I had first seen her I had thought her small and silent. Now she was smaller and dreadfully still. I felt Mark push past me, entering the room.

"Is she...?" he began.

"Yes," Tim said. "She's asleep."

"I don't think so, Tim," I said.

Eric went over to her and took her wrist between a podgy finger and thumb. "She has no pulse," he said. He leant over her. "She's not breathing."

Tim's mouth fell open. "Do you think she's ill?" he asked.

"She's dead, Tim," I said. Two murders in one day. And it wasn't even Tim's bedtime.

Libby burst into tears. It was getting to be a habit with her. At least Brenda didn't scream again. At this close range, I'm not sure my eardrums could have taken it.

"What are we going to do?" someone asked. I wasn't sure who it was and it didn't matter anyway. Because right then I didn't have any idea.

"It might have been a heart attack," Tim said. "Maybe the shock of what happened to Rory..."

Darkness had fallen on Crocodile Island. It

189

had slithered across the surface of the sea and thrown itself over the house. Now and then a full moon came out from behind the clouds and for a moment the waves would ripple silver before disappearing into inky blackness. Tim and I were sitting on our four-poster bed. It looked like we were going to have to share it. Two posters each.

Maybe it had been a heart attack. Maybe she had died of fright. Maybe she'd caught a very bad case of flu. Everyone had their own ideas ... but I knew better. I remembered the twist of silver I had seen on the carpet.

"Tim, what can you tell me about Sylvie Binns?" I asked.

"Not a lot." Tim fell silent. "She was good at chemistry."

"I know that."

"She used to go out with Mark. We always thought the two of them would get married, but in the end she met someone else. Mark ran all the way round England. That was his way of forgetting her."

Mark Tyler had been the last person to see Sylvie alive. I wondered if he really had forgotten her. Or forgiven her.

"Maybe she was ill before she came to the island," Tim muttered.

"Tim, I think she was poisoned," I said.

"Poisoned?"

I remembered my first sight of Sylvie, on the

quay. She had been eating a chocolate flake. "Sylvie liked sweets and chocolate," I said.

"You're right, Nick! Yes. She loved chocolate. She could never resist it. When Mark was going out with her, he took her on a tour of a chocolate factory. She even ate the tickets." Tim frowned. "But what's that got to do with anything?"

"There was a piece of silver paper on the floor in her room. I think it was the wrapper off a sweet or a chocolate. Don't you see? Someone knew she couldn't resist chocolate – so they left one in her room. Maybe on her pillow."

"And it wasn't almond crunch," Tim muttered darkly.

"More likely cyanide surprise," I said.

We got into bed. Tim didn't want to turn off the lights, but a few minutes later, after he had dozed off, I reached for the switch and lay back in the darkness. I needed to think. Sylvie had eaten a poisoned chocolate. I was sure of it. But had she been given it or had she found it in her room? If it was already in the room, it could have been left there before we arrived. But if she had been given it, then the killer must still be on the island. He or she might even be in the house.

There was a movement at the window.

At first I thought I'd imagined it, but propping myself up in the bed, I saw it again. There was somebody there! No – that was impossible.

191

We were on the first floor. Then I remembered. There was a terrace running round the outside of the house, connecting all the bedrooms.

There it was again. I stared in horror. There was a face staring at me from the other side of the glass, a hideous skull with hollow eyes and grinning, tombstone teeth. The bones glowed in the moonlight. Now I'll be honest with you. I don't scare easily. But right then I was frozen. I couldn't move. I couldn't cry out. I'm almost surprised I didn't wet the bed.

The skull hovered in front of me. I couldn't see a body. It had to be draped in black. It's a mask, I told myself. Someone is trying to frighten you with a joke-shop mask. Somehow, I managed to force back the fear. I jerked up in bed and threw back the covers. Next to me, Tim woke up.

"Is it breakfast already?" he asked.

I ignored him. I was already darting towards the window. But at that moment, the moon vanished behind another cloud and the darkness fell. By the time I had found the lock and opened the window, the man – or woman, whoever it was – had gone.

"What is it, Nick?" Tim demanded.

I didn't answer. But it seemed that whoever had killed Rory McDougal and Sylvie Binns was still on the island.

Which left me wondering – who was going to be next?

SEARCH PARTY

Janet Rhodes didn't make it to breakfast.

There were just the five of us, sitting in the kitchen with five bowls of Frosties and a steaming plate of scrambled eggs that Brenda had insisted on cooking but which nobody felt like eating. Libby had another cigarette in her mouth but everyone had complained so much that she wasn't smoking it. She was sucking it. Eric was still in his dressing-gown, a thick red thing with his initials – ED – embroidered on the pocket. Mark was wearing a track suit. A security camera winked at us from one corner of the room. There were a lot of security cameras on the island. But none of us felt even slightly secure.

"What are we going to do?" Brenda asked. I got the feeling that she hadn't slept very much the night before. There were dark rings under her eyes and although she'd put on lipstick, most of it had missed her lips. "This island is haunted!" she went on.

"What do you mean?" Eric asked.

"Last night ... my window ... it was horrible."

"I've got quite a nice window," Tim said.

"I mean ... I saw something! A human skull. It was dancing in the night air."

So she'd seen it too! I was about to chip in, but then Eric interrupted. "I don't think it's going to help, sharing our bad dreams," he said.

"I didn't dream it," Brenda insisted.

"We've got to do something!" Mark cut in. "First Rory, then Sylvie. At this rate, there won't be any of us left by lunch-time."

"I don't want any lunch," Libby muttered.

"We need to talk about this," Eric said. "We need to work something out. But there's no point starting until we're all here." He glanced at the clock. "Where the hell is Janet?"

"Maybe she's in the bath," Tim suggested.

"In the water or underneath it?" Eric growled.

The minute hand on the kitchen clock ticked forward. It was nine o'clock. Suddenly Mark stood up. "I'm going upstairs," he announced.

"You're going back to bed?" Tim asked.

"I'm going to find her."

He left the room. The rest of us followed

him, tiptoeing up the stairs and along the corridor with a sense of dread. Actually, Eric didn't exactly tiptoe. He was so fat that it must have been quite a few years since his toes *had* tips. Mark Tyler had moved quickly, taking the stairs four at a time as if they were hurdles and he was back at the Olympic games at Atlanta. He was outside the door when we arrived.

"She's overslept," Tim said to me. "She's fine. She's just overslept."

Eric knocked on her door. There was no answer. He knocked again, then turned the handle. The door opened.

The hairdresser had overslept all right, but nothing was ever going to wake her up again. She had been stabbed during the night. She was lying on her back on a four-poster bed like the one in our room, only smaller. The bed was old. The paint had peeled off the posts and there was a tear in the canopy above her. In fact the whole room looked shabby, as if it had been missed out by the decorators. Maybe I noticed all this because I didn't want to look at the body. You may think I'm crazy, but dead people upset me. And when I did finally look at her, I got a shock.

Whoever had killed her hadn't used a knife. There was something sticking out of her chest and at first I thought it was some sort of rocket. It was silver, in the shape of a sort of long pyramid, with four legs jutting out. Then, slowly, it dawned on me what I was looking at. It was a model, a souvenir of the building that I had climbed up with Tim only the year before.

It was incredible. But true. Janet Rhodes had been stabbed with a model of the Eiffel Tower.

"The Eiffel Tower!" Tim muttered. His face was the colour of sour milk. "It's an outrage. I mean, it's meant to be a tourist attraction!"

"Why the Eiffel Tower?" I asked.

"Because it's famous, Nick. People like to visit it."

"No – I don't mean, why is it a tourist attraction. I mean, why use it as a murder weapon? It's certainly a strange choice. Maybe someone is trying to tell us something."

"Well, they certainly told Janet something," Tim said.

We were back at the breakfast table. The scrambled eggs were cold and congealed and looked even less appetizing than before. All the Frosties had gone soggy. But it didn't matter. There was no way anybody was going to eat anything today. The way things were going, I wondered if any of us would ever eat anything again.

Nobody was talking very much. I knew why. But it was Brenda who put it into words.

"Do you realize…" she began, and for once

her voice was hoarse and empty. "Do you realize that the killer could be sitting here, at this table."

Tim looked around. "But there's only us here!"

"That's what she means, Tim," I said. "She's saying that the killer could be one of us!"

Brenda nodded. "I know it's one of us. One of us got up last night and went down the corridor." She shuddered. "I thought I heard squeaking last night…"

"That was Tim," I said. "He snores."

"No. It was a floorboard. Somebody left their room…"

"Did anyone else hear anything last night?" Eric asked.

There was a pause. Then Libby nodded. "I have the room next to Mark," she said. She turned to look at him. "I heard your door open just after midnight. I heard you go into the corridor."

"I went to the toilet," Mark replied. His dark face had suddenly got darker. He didn't like being accused.

"You went to the toilet in the corridor?" Tim asked.

"I went to the toilet which is across the corridor, opposite my room. I didn't go anywhere near Janet."

"What about the skull?" Brenda whispered.

Eric scowled. He had forgotten about the dancing skull. "I know you say it's a dream, Eric," she went on. "But that's typical of you. You never believed anything I said, even when we were at school. Well, believe me now..." she took a deep breath. "Maybe it wasn't a ghost or a monster. Maybe it was someone in a mask. But they were there! I was awake. I jumped out of bed and went over to the window but by the time I got there, seconds later, they'd gone. Vanished into thin air..."

"It wasn't a dream," I said. "I saw it too."

"You?" Eric sneered at me.

I nodded.

"I didn't see anything," Tim said.

"You were asleep, Tim. But it was definitely there. It came out of nowhere ... like a magic trick. A rabbit out of a hat!"

"You saw a rabbit too?" Tim asked.

We all ignored him. "Any one of us could have climbed out onto the terrace," Brenda said. "Any one of us could have killed Janet. And Rory. And Sylvie! How do we know that she wasn't strangled or poisoned or something?"

"I think she *was* poisoned," I said.

Everyone looked at me so I told them about the sweet wrapper and Sylvie's love of chocolate. It was strange. Everyone in the room was ten years older than me but suddenly I was in control.

Not for long, though. Eric Draper, the ex-head boy, raised his hands. "Ladies and gentlemen," he announced. "I don't think we should jump to conclusions. Why would any of us sitting at this table want to kill Rory or Sylvie or Janet?"

"Mark used to go out with Sylvie," Libby said. She was staring at him. "When she broke up with you, you told me you wanted to kill her."

"That was ten years ago!" Mark protested. He jerked a finger at Libby. "Anyway, what about *you*? You nearly *did* kill Rory with that bicycle pump..."

"Yes. And what about you!" Tim pointed at Eric. "You say your name's Eric, so why are you wearing a dressing-gown that belongs to Ed?"

It took Eric a few seconds to work out what Tim was getting at. "Those are my initials, you idiot!" he snapped. He took a deep breath and raised his hands. "Look," he went on. "There's no point arguing amongst ourselves. We have to stick together. It could be our only hope."

The others fell silent. I had to admit, Eric was speaking sense. Blaming each other wouldn't help.

"Both Brenda and ... Tim's little brother saw somebody last night," he went on. I didn't know why he couldn't call me by my name.

"Now that could have been one of us, dressing up to frighten the others. But remember, we were all inside the house … and this thing, whatever it was, was outside. So maybe it was someone else. Maybe it was someone we don't know about."

"You mean … someone hiding on the island?" Mark said.

"Exactly. We know we can't call the police. We know we're stuck here. But it seems to me that the first thing we have to do is find out if there's anyone else here."

"We've got to organize a search party," I said.

Tim shook his head. "This is no time for a party, Nick," he muttered.

"You're right, Eric," Libby said. "We've got to go over the island from head to tail."

"But at the same time, I think we should keep an eye on each other," Brenda said. "I'll feel safer that way."

Eric went upstairs to get changed. Mark went with him. From now on, we were going to do everything in pairs. Brenda and Libby cleared the breakfast things. I'd already noticed that most of the food in the house was in tins – which was just as well. Even the cleverest killer couldn't tamper with a tin, so at least we wouldn't starve. At half past nine we all met in the hall. Then we put on our coats and went outside.

The search began back at the jetty, right at the head of the crocodile. The idea was that we could cover the entire island, working like the police searching a wood when someone has gone missing. That is, we kept ten metres apart, always in sight of one another, moving across the island in a line. It was a beautiful day. The sun was shining and the sea was blue, but even so I could feel a chill breeze on Crocodile Island. And there was something else. I couldn't escape the feeling that I was being watched. It was weird. Because it was obvious that there wasn't anybody in sight ... not even so much as a sheep or a cow.

It only took us an hour to cover the island. There really wasn't very much there. Most of it was covered in gorse that only came up to the knee, which no killer could have hidden behind – unless, of course, he happened to be extremely small. There were a few trees but we checked the branches and Tim even climbed one to see if anyone was hiding at the top. Then I climbed up to help Tim down again and we moved on. We came to a couple of ruined outbuildings. I went inside. There was nobody there – but I did see something. Another security camera, fixed to the brickwork. Of course, a rich man like Rory would have had to be careful about security. I remembered the camera I had noticed in the kitchen. He had probably covered the whole island. Was that why I had felt we were being watched?

We went past the house and continued towards the crocodile's tail. The ground rose steeply up, finally arriving at a narrow point at least twenty metres above the sea. This was what I had seen from the boat. Six great rocks, steel grey and needle-sharp, rose out of the water far below. Looking down made my head spin. I wondered briefly if there might be a cave somewhere, perhaps tucked underneath the lip where we were standing. But then a wave rolled in, crashing against the cliff face. If there was a killer down there, he'd be soaking wet. And anyway, as far as I could see, there was no way down.

We moved away, retracing our steps. There was nobody outside the house, but how about inside? Starting in the hall, we went from room to room: the library, the dining-room, the conservatory, the hall and so on. We looked behind curtains, under tables, in the fireplaces and up the chimneys. Tim even looked in the grandfather clocks. Maybe he thought he'd find somebody's grandfather. We covered the ground floor and then went up to the first. Here were the bedrooms, with our names still attached to the doors. We went into every one of them. There was nobody there ... apart from the three very dead bodies. It wasn't easy searching those particular rooms, but we made ourselves ... although I think Tim was wasting

202

his time doing it with his eyes tightly shut.

Nobody in the rooms. Nobody in the corridors. We found the attic but all that was there was a water tank. Tim dipped his head in and I made a mental note not to drink any more water. Not with his dandruff. Eventually, we gave up. We had been everywhere. There was nowhere else to look.

We started to go back down to the kitchen but had only got halfway there when Libby let out a little gasp.

"What is it?" Eric demanded.

"There." She pointed at the wall at the end of the corridor. "I don't know why I didn't see it before!"

What she had seen was a black-and-white photograph in a silver frame. It was hanging right in the middle of the wall with enough space around it to make it stand out. The question was – had Rory hung it there? Or had it been someone else? Was this something we were meant to see?

The photograph showed nine teenagers, all of them wearing the same uniform. It's funny how people change in ten years – but I recognized them at once: Eric Draper, Janet Rhodes, Mark Tyler, Brenda Blake, Sylvie Binns, Libby Goldman, Rory McDougal and Tim. Tim looked the weirdest of them all. He'd had long hair then, and spots. Lots of spots. Of course, I wouldn't have looked too great myself when the picture had been taken – but then I would only have been four years old.

There was one face, however, that I didn't know. He was standing at the edge of the group, slightly apart; a thin, gangly teenager with curly hair and glasses. He was wearing an anorak and had the sort of face you'd expect to see on a train-spotter. "Who's he?" I asked.

"That's Johnny!" Brenda replied. "Johnny Nadler. He was one of my best friends…"

"And mine," Libby agreed. "Everyone liked Johnny. We used to hang out with him in the yard." She walked closer to the photograph. "I remember when this was taken. It was prize-giving day. He came second in geography. I came first."

"Wait a minute," I interrupted. "Everyone in this photograph is here on Crocodile Island. Everyone except Johnny Nadler!"

"You're right!" Mark agreed. "Why wasn't he invited?"

"Because he's the killer!" Eric snapped. "He's got to be!"

"But why would Johnny want to kill Rory?" Brenda asked. "The two of them were friends. And every day after school he used to catch the bus with Sylvie – even though it took him eight miles in the wrong direction. That's how much he liked her."

"He let Janet cut his hair," Libby went on. "She accidentally cut a chunk out of his ear,

204

but he didn't mind. In fact he laughed all the way to the hospital. Johnny wouldn't hurt anyone."

"What else can you tell me about him?" I asked.

"He came second in history as well as geography," Eric said. "He was really clever."

"He was always playing with model planes and cars," Mark added. "He used to build them himself. We always said he'd be an inventor when he left school but in fact he ended up working at Boots. I saw him there once, when I went in to get some ointment." He blushed. "I had athlete's foot."

"Did any of the rest of you ever see him again?" I asked.

Everyone shook their heads. I looked at the photograph again. It did seem strange that he was the only one in the picture who hadn't been invited to Crocodile Island. But did that make him the killer? And if so, where on earth was he? We had searched the entire island and we were certain now that we were the only ones who were there.

Eric looked at his watch. It was half past twelve. "I suggest we continue this meeting downstairs," he said.

"I need to change," Brenda said.

"Me too," Libby agreed.

Everyone started to move in different directions.

"Hold on a minute!" I said. "I thought we were all going to stick together. I think we should all stay in this room."

"Don't be ridiculous!" Eric snapped. "We have to eat something. It's lunch-time. And anyway, we've just searched the island. We know there's nobody else here."

"Well, I'm staying with Tim," I said.

"How do you know I'm not the killer?" Tim demanded.

Because whoever killed Rory and the others is brilliant and fiendish and you still have trouble tying your shoelaces. That was what I thought, but I didn't say anything. I just shrugged.

"I don't want to be near anyone," Libby said. "I feel safer on my own."

"Me too." Brenda nodded. "And I'm certainly not having anyone in the room with me while I'm changing."

"We can meet in ten minutes," Eric said. "We're inside the house. We know there's nobody else on the island. We'll meet in the dining-room at twenty to one."

He was wrong of course. This was one little group that was never going to meet again. But how could we know that? We were scared and we weren't thinking straight.

Tim and I went back to our room. Tim scratched his head, which was still damp from the water tank. "Johnny could be hiding on

206

the island," he said. "What if there's a secret room?"

The same thought had already occurred to me, but I'd tapped every wall and every wooden panel and nothing had sounded hollow. "I don't think there are any secret rooms, Tim," I said.

"But you can't be sure..." Tim began to tap his way along the wall, his eyes half-closed, listening for a hollow sound. A few moments later, he straightened up, excited. "There's definitely something on the other side here!" he cried.

"I know, Tim," I said. "That's the window."

I left him in the bedroom, drying his hair, and went back downstairs. I was going to join the others in the dining-room. But I never got that far. I was about halfway down when I heard it. A short, sudden scream. Then a crashing sound. It had come from somewhere outside.

I ran down the rest of the way, through the hall and out the front door. Mark Tyler appeared, running round the side of the house.

"What was it...?" he demanded. He was trying not to sound scared but it wasn't working.

"Round the back?"

We went there together, moving more slowly now, knowing what we were going to find, not wanting to find it. The kitchen door opened and Brenda Blake came out. I noticed she was breathing heavily.

This time it was Libby Goldman. I'm afraid she had recorded her last episode of *Libby's Lounge* and for her the final credits were already rolling. Why had she gone outside? Maybe she'd decided to light up one of her cigarettes – in which case, this was one time when smoking certainly had been bad for her health. Fatal, in fact. But it hadn't been the tobacco that had killed her. Something had hit her hard on the head: something that had been dropped from above. I looked up, working out the angles. We were directly underneath the battlements. Behind them, the roof was flat. It would have been easy enough for someone to hide up there, to wait for any one of us to step outside. Libby must have come out to get a breath of fresh air before the meeting. Air wasn't something she'd be needing again.

There were footsteps on the gravel. Eric and Tim had arrived. They stared in silence. Mark stretched out a finger and pointed. It took me a minute to work out what he was pointing at. That was how much his finger was trembling.

And there it was, lying in the grass. At first I didn't recognize the object that had been dropped from the roof and which had fallen right onto Libby Goldman. I mean, I knew what it was – but I couldn't believe that that was what had been used.

It was a big round ball: a globe. The sort of thing you find in a library. Maybe it had been in Rory's library before the killer had carried it up to the roof. The United States of America was facing up. It was stained red.

I looked at Eric Draper. His mouth had dropped open. He looked genuinely shocked. Mark Tyler was standing opposite him, staring. Brenda Blake was to one side. She was crying.

One of them had to be faking it. I was certain of it. One of them had to have climbed down from the room after watching Libby fall. There was nobody else here. One of them had to be the killer.

But which one?

MORE MURDER

Eric Draper? Brenda Blake? Or Mark Tyler?

It was early evening and Tim and I had gone for a walk – supposedly to clear our heads. But the truth was, I wanted to be alone with him and somehow I felt safer away from the house. It struck me that all the deaths had taken place inside or near the building. And if we stayed too close to the house something else might strike me – a falling piano or a model of the Taj Mahal, for example.

I glanced down at the piece of paper I was holding in my hand. I had made a few notes just before we left:

RORY McDOUGAL – Killed with a sword.
SYLVIE BINNS – Poisoned.
JANET RHODES – Stabbed with an Eiffel Tower!

LIBBY GOLDMAN – Knocked down with a globe.

There was a pattern in there somewhere but I just couldn't see it. Maybe some fresh air would help after all.

"I've got an idea!" Tim said.

"Go ahead, Tim," I said.

"Maybe I could swim back over to the coast and get some help."

We were sitting on the jetty. Today the sea was flat, the waves caught as if in a photograph. I could just make out the mainland, a vague ribbon lying on the horizon. The sun was setting fast. How many of us would see it rise again?

I shook my head. "No, Tim. It's too far."

"It can't be more than five miles."

"And you can't swim."

"Oh yes. I'd forgotten." He glanced at me. "But you can."

"I can't swim five miles!" I said. "The water's too cold. And there's too much of it. No. Our only hope is to solve this before the killer strikes again."

"You're right, Nick." Tim closed his eyes and sat in silence for a minute. Then he opened them again. "Maybe we could get one of the others to swim..."

"One of the others *is* the killer!" I said. "I saw someone out on the terrace, wearing a

211

skeleton mask. I don't know how they managed to disappear so quickly – but I wasn't imagining it. Brenda saw them too."

"Maybe it was Mark! He's a fast mover."

"And just now ... when Libby Goldman was killed. Someone must have climbed up onto the roof." I thought back. "Brenda was out of breath when she came into the garden..."

"She could have been singing!"

"I doubt it. But she could have been running. She drops the globe, then runs all the way downstairs..."

A seagull flew overhead, crying mournfully. I knew how it felt. I almost wanted to cry myself.

"What's missing is the motive," I went on. "Think back, Tim. You were at school with these people. There are only three of them left – Brenda, Mark and Eric. Would any of them have any reason to kill the rest of you?"

Tim sighed. "The only people who ever threatened to kill me," he said, "were the teachers. My French teacher once threw a piece of chalk at me. And when that missed, he threw the blackboard."

"How did you get on with Mark Tyler?"

"We were friends. We used to play conkers together." He scratched his head. "I did once miss his conker and break three of his fingers, but I don't think he minded too much."

"How about Brenda Blake?"

Tim thought back. "She was in the school choir," he said. "She was also in the rugby team. She used to sing in the scrum." He scratched his head. "We used to tease her a bit but it was never serious."

"Maybe she didn't agree."

The waves rolled in towards us. I looked out at the mainland, hoping to catch sight of Horatio Randle and his boat, the *Silver Medal*. But the sea was empty, darkening as the sun dipped behind it. What had the old fisherman said when he'd dropped us? *"I'll be back in a couple of days."* It had been Wednesday when we arrived. He might not return until the weekend. How many passengers would there be left waiting for him?

"How about Eric Draper?" I asked.

"What about him?"

"He could be the killer. It would have to be someone strong to carry the globe up to the roof in the first place. Can you remember anything about him?"

Tim laughed. "He was a great sport. I'll never forget the last day of term when the seven of us pulled off his trousers and threw him in the canal!"

"What?" I exclaimed. "You pulled off his trousers and threw him in the canal? Why?"

"Well, he was the head boy. And he'd always been bossy. It was just a bit of fun. Except that he nearly drowned. And the canal was so polluted, he had to spend six months in hospital."

"Are you telling me that the seven of you nearly killed Eric?" I was almost screaming. "Hasn't it occurred to you that this whole thing could be his revenge?"

"But it was just a joke!"

"You almost killed him, Tim! Maybe he wasn't amused."

I stood up. It was time to go back to the house. The other three would be waiting for us … if they'd managed to survive the last half-hour.

"I wish I'd never come here," Tim muttered.

"I wish you'd never come here," I agreed.

"Poor Libby. And Sylvie. And Janet. And Rory, of course. He was first."

We walked a few more steps in silence. Then I suddenly stopped. "What did you say, Tim?" I demanded.

"I didn't say anything!"

"Yes, you did! Before you weren't saying anything, you were saying something."

"I asked which side of the bed you wanted."

"No. That was yesterday." I played back what he had just said and that was when I saw it, the pattern I'd been looking for. "You're brilliant!" I said.

"Thanks!" Tim frowned. "What have I done?"

"Tell me," I said. "Did Libby come first

214

in anything at school? And was it … by any chance … geography?"

"Yes. She did. How did you know?"

"Let's get back inside," I said.

I found Eric, Mark and Brenda in the drawing-room. This was one of the most extraordinary rooms in the house – almost like a chapel with a great stained glass window at one end and a high, vaulted ceiling. Rory McDougal had obviously fancied himself as a musician. There was even a church organ against the wall, the silver pipes looming over us. Like so many of the other rooms, the walls were lined with old weapons. In here they were antique pistols; muskets and flintlocks. All in all, we couldn't have chosen a worse house to share with a mass murderer. There were more weapons than you'd find in the Tower of London and I just hoped that they weren't as real as they looked.

The three survivors were sitting in heavy, leather chairs. I stood in front of them with the organ on one side and a row of bookshelves on the other. Everyone was watching me and I felt a bit like Hercule Poirot at the end of one of his cases, explaining it to the suspects. The only trouble was, this wasn't the end of the case. I was still certain that I was talking to the murderer. He or she had to be one of the people in the room.

Somewhere outside, a clock chimed the

hour. It was nine o'clock. Night had fallen.

"Seven of you were invited to Crocodile Island," I began. "And I see now that you all have something in common."

"We went to the same school," interrupted Tim.

"I know that, Tim. But there's something else. You all got prizes for coming first. You've already told me that Rory was first in maths. Libby was first in geography..."

"What's this got to do with anything?" Eric snapped.

"Don't you see? Libby was first in geography and someone dropped a globe on her head. Someone told me that Sylvie Binns came first in chemistry and we think she was poisoned."

"Janet came first in French..." Mark murmured.

"...which would explain why she was stabbed with a model of the Eiffel Tower. And Rory McDougal came first in maths."

"He was stabbed too," Eric said.

"He was more than stabbed. He was divided!"

There was a long silence.

"That's the reason why Johnny Nadler wasn't invited to the island," Brenda said. "He never came first in anything. He was second..."

"But that means..." Eric had gone pale. "I came first in history."

216

"I came first in sport," Mark said.

Brenda nodded. "And I came first in music."

We all turned to look at Tim. But he couldn't have come first in anything … could he? I noticed he was blushing. He licked his lips and looked the other way.

"What did you come first in, Tim?" I asked.

"I didn't…" he began, but I could tell he was lying.

"We have to know," I said. "It could be important."

"I remember…" Brenda began.

"All right," Tim sighed. "I got first prize in needlework."

"Needlework!" I exclaimed.

"Well … yes. It was a hobby of mine. Just for a bit. I mean…" He was going redder and redder. "I didn't even want the prize. I just got it. It was for a handkerchief…"

The idea of my sixteen-year-old brother winning a prize for an embroidered hanky made my head spin. But this wasn't the time to laugh. Hopefully I'd be able to do that later.

"Wait a minute! Wait a minute!" Eric said. He looked annoyed. Maybe it was because I was ten years younger than him and I was the one who'd worked it out. "I came first in history – and you're saying I'm going to be killed … *historically?*"

"That's what it looks like," I said.

"But how…?"

I pointed at the wall, at the flintlock pistols on the wooden plaques. "Maybe someone will use one of those," I said. "Or there are swords, arrows, spears ... that bear upstairs is even holding a blunderbuss. This place is full of old weapons."

"What about me?" Brenda whispered.

"You're not an old weapon!" Tim said.

"I came first in music." Brenda glared at the organ as if it was about to jump off the wall and eat her.

"But who's *doing* this?" Mark cut in. "I mean ... it's got to be someone in this room. Right? We know there's nobody else on the island. There can't be anybody hiding. We've searched everywhere."

"It's him!" Brenda pointed at Eric. "He never forgave us for throwing him in the canal. This is his revenge!"

"What about *you?*" Eric returned. "You once said you were going to kill us all. It was in the school yard. I remember it clearly!"

"That's true!" Mark said.

"You used to bully me all the time," Brenda wailed. "Just because I had pigtails. And crooked teeth."

"And you were fat," Tim reminded her.

"But I didn't mean it, when I said that." She turned to Mark. "You said you were going to kill Tim when he broke all your fingers with that conker!"

"I only broke three of them!" Tim interrupted.

"I didn't much like Tim," Mark agreed. "And you're right. I would have quite happily strangled him. Not that it would have been easy with three broken fingers. But I never had any argument with you or with Eric or any of the others. Why would I want to kill you?"

"It's still got to be one of us," Eric insisted. He paused. "It can't be Tim," he went on.

"Why not?" Tim asked.

"Because this whole business is the work of a fiendish madman and you're not fiendish. You're just silly!"

"Oh thanks!" Tim looked away.

"I know it's not me..." Eric went on.

"That's what you say," Brenda sniffed.

"I know it's not me, so it's got to be Brenda or Mark."

"What about Sylvie?" Tim suggested.

"She's already dead, Tim," I reminded him, quietly.

"Oh yes."

"This is all irrelevant," Mark said. "The question is – what are we going to do? We could be stuck on this island for days, or even weeks. It all depends on when Captain Randle comes back. And by then it could be too late!"

"I'd like to make a suggestion," I said. Everyone stopped and looked at me. "The first thing is, we've all got to keep each other in sight."

"The kid's right," Mark agreed. "So long as we can see each other, we're going to be safe."

"That's true!" Tim exclaimed. "All we have to do is keep our eyes open and everything will be fine." He turned to me. "You're brilliant, Nick. For a moment there I was getting really worried."

Then all the lights went out.

It happened so suddenly that for a moment I thought it was just me. Had I been knocked out or somehow closed my eyes without noticing? The last thing I saw was the four of them – Eric, Brenda, Mark and Tim – sitting in their chairs as if caught in a photograph. Then everything was black. There was no moon that night and even if there had been the stained glass window would have kept most of the light out. Darkness came crashing onto us. It was total.

"Don't panic!" Eric said.

There was a gunshot. I saw it, a spark of red on the other side of the room.

Tim screamed and for a horrible moment I wondered if he had been shot. I forced myself to calm down. He'd come first in needlework. Nobody would be aiming a gun at him.

"Tim!" I called out.

"Can I panic now?" he called back.

"Eric…?" That was Mark's voice.

And then there was a sort of groaning sound, followed by a heavy thud. At the same time I heard a door open and close. I stood up, trying to see through the darkness. But it was hopeless. I couldn't even make out my own hand in front of my face.

"Tim?" I called again.

"Nick?" I was relieved to hear his voice.

"Eric?" I tried.

Silence.

"Brenda?"

Nothing.

"Mark?"

The lights came back on.

There were only two people alive in the room. I was standing in front of my chair. One more step and I'd have put my foot through the coffee table. Tim was *under* the coffee table. He must have crawled there when the lights went out. Eric was on the floor. He had been shot. There was a flintlock pistol, still smoking, lying on the carpet on the other side of the room. It must have been taken off the wall, fired and then dropped. At least, that's what it looked like. Brenda was sitting in her chair. She was dead too. One of the organ pipes – the largest – had been pulled down on top of her. That must have been the thud I had heard. Brenda had sung her last opera. The only music she needed now was a hymn.

There was no sign of Mark.

"Are you all right, Tim?" I demanded.

"Yes!" Tim sounded surprised. "I haven't been murdered!" he exclaimed.

"I noticed." I waited while he climbed out from underneath the coffee table. "At least we know who the killer is," I said.

"Do we?"

"It's got to be Mark," I said. "Mark Tyler..."

"I always knew it was him," Tim said. "Call it intuition. Call it experience. But I knew he was a killer even before he'd done any killing."

"I don't know, Tim," I said. It bothered me, because to be honest Mark was the last person I would have suspected. And yet, at the same time, I had to admit ... it would have taken a fast mover to push the globe off the roof and make it all the way downstairs in time and Mark was the fastest person on the island.

"Where do you think he went?" Tim asked.

"I don't know."

We left the room carefully. In fact, Tim made me leave it first. The fact was that – unless I'd got the whole thing wrong – it was just the three of us now on the island; Mark could be waiting for us anywhere. Or waiting for Tim, rather. He had no quarrel with me. And that made me think. Tim had come first in needlework. Following the pattern of the other deaths, that meant he would probably be killed with some sort of needle. But what would that mean? A sewing needle dipped in poison? A hypodermic syringe?

Tim must have had the same thought. He was looking everywhere, afraid to touch anything, afraid even to take another step. We went out into the hall. The fire had died down and was glowing red. The front door was open.

"Maybe he went outside," Tim said.

"What would be the point?" I asked.

Tim shuddered. "Don't talk about points," he said.

We went outside. And that was where we found Mark. He had come first in sport but now he had reached the finishing line. Somebody had been throwing the javelin and they'd thrown it at him. It had hit him in the chest. He was lying on the grass, doing a good impersonation of a sausage on a stick.

"It's ... it's ... it's..." Tim couldn't finish the sentence.

"Yeah," I said. "It's Mark." There were a few leaves scattered around his body. That puzzled me. The nearest trees were ten metres away. But this wasn't the time to play the detective. There were no more suspects. And only one more victim.

I looked at Tim.

Tim looked at me.

We were the only two left.

NEEDLES

Tim didn't sleep well that night. Although I hadn't said anything, not wanting to upset him, even he had managed to work out that he had to be the next on the killer's list. He also knew that his own murder would have something to do with needlework. So he was looking for needles everywhere.

By one o'clock in the morning we knew that there were no sewing needles in the room, no knitting needles and no pine needles. Even so, it took him an hour to get into bed and several more hours to get to sleep. Mind you, nobody would have found it easy getting to sleep dressed in a full suit of medieval armour, but that still hadn't stopped Tim putting it on.

"There could be a poisoned needle in the mattress," he said. "Or someone could try and inject me with a syringe."

Tim didn't snore that night; he clanked.

224

Every time he rolled over he sounded like twenty cans of beans in a washing machine. I just hoped he wasn't planning to take a bath in the suit of armour the following morning. That way he could end up rusting to death.

At four-thirty, he woke up screaming.

"What is it, Tim?" I asked.

"I had a bad dream, Nick," he said.

"Don't tell me. You saw a needle."

"No. I saw a haystack."

I didn't sleep well either. I got cramp and woke up in the morning with pins and needles. I didn't tell Tim, though. He'd have had a fit.

We had breakfast together in the kitchen. Neither of us ate very much. For a start, we were surrounded by dead bodies, which didn't make us feel exactly cheerful. But Tim was also terrified. I'd managed to persuade him to change out of the armour but now he was worrying about the food. Were there going to be needles in the cereal? A needle in the tea? In the end, I gave him a straw with a tissue sellotaped over the end. The tissue worked as a filter and he was able to suck up a little orange juice and a very softly-boiled egg.

I have to say that for once I was baffled. It was still like being in an Agatha Christie novel – only this time I couldn't flick through to the last page and see who did it without bothering to read the rest. Personally, I had always thought Eric had been the killer. He seemed to have the strongest motive – being half-drowned on the last day of school. It was funny really. All eight of the old boys and girls of St Egbert's had disliked each other. But someone, somewhere, had disliked them all even more. The whole thing had been planned right down to the last detail. And the last detail, unfortunately, was Tim.

But who? And why?

Tim sat miserably at his end of the table, hardly daring to move. Why had he had to come first in *needlework* of all things? How was I supposed to find the needle that was going to kill him? I knew now that the only hope for me was to solve this thing before the killer struck one last time. And a nasty thought had already occurred to me. Would the killer stop with Tim? I wasn't meant to be part of this. I had never gone to St Egbert's. But I was a witness to what had happened and maybe I had seen too much.

I went over what had happened last night. We had always assumed that there was nobody else on the island, but thinking it through I knew this couldn't be true. We had all been sitting down: Brenda in front of the organ, Eric opposite her, Mark nearest the door and Tim and me on the sofa. But none of us had been anywhere near the light switch, and someone had most certainly turned off the lights – not just in the drawing-room but throughout the entire house. Somewhere down in the basement, there would be a main fuse switch. But that led to another question. If the killer had been down in the basement, then how had he or she managed to appear in the room seconds later to shoot Eric and push the organ pipe onto Brenda?

At the time, I had assumed that Mark had committed the last two murders. There had been a shot, then a thud, then the opening and closing of a door. But a few seconds later, Mark had himself been killed. And what about the leaves that I had seen lying next to his body? How had they got there?

I thought back to the other murders. Rory first. We had all been on the island and we had all separated. Any one of us could have attacked him and, immediately afterwards, left the chocolate on the bed for Sylvie to find. That was the night I had seen the face at the window. A face that had appeared and disappeared – impossibly – in seconds. And then we had found Janet. I remembered her lying in her bed, stabbed by a model of the Eiffel Tower. Her room had been shabby. There had been a tear in the canopy ... I had remarked on it at the time. Why had it caught my eye?

Libby Goldman next. The television presenter had been knocked down with a model globe. There was something strange about that, too. Someone must have carried it up to the roof and dropped it on her when she came out of the front door. But now that I thought about it, I hadn't seen the globe in any of the rooms when we had been searching the house. And that could only mean one thing. It had been on the roof from the very start, waiting for her...

Maybe you know how it is when you've been given a particularly nasty piece of home-work – an impossible equation or a fiendish bit of physics or something. You stare at it and stare at it, but it's all just ink on paper and you're about to give up when you notice something and suddenly you realize it's not so difficult after all. Well, that was what was happening to me now.

I remembered the search party, slowly criss-crossing the island. We had seen security cameras everywhere and from the day I had arrived, I had felt that I was being watched. There was a security camera in the kitchen. I looked up. It was watching me even now. Were there cameras in other rooms, too?

At the same time, I remembered something Mark had said, when we had found the old photograph of St Egbert's. And in that second, as quickly as that, I suddenly knew everything.

"I've got it, Tim!" I said.

"So have I, Nick!" Tim cried.

I'd been so wrapped up in my own thoughts, that I hadn't noticed Tim had been thinking too. Now he was staring at me with the sort of look you see on a fish when it's spent too long out of water.

"You know who did it?" I asked.

"Yes."

"Go on!"

"It's simple!" Tim explained. "First there were eight of us on the island, then seven, then six, then five..."

"I know," I interrupted. "I can count backwards."

"Well, now there are only two of us left. I know it wasn't me who committed the murders." He reached forward and snatched up a spoon. Then he realized what he'd done, put it down and snatched up a knife. He waved it at me. "So the killer must be you!" he exclaimed.

"What?" I couldn't believe what I was hearing.

"There's only us left. You and me. I know it wasn't me so it must have been you."

"But why would I want to kill everyone?" I demanded.

"You tell me!"

"I wouldn't! And I didn't! Don't be ridiculous, Tim."

I stood up. That was a mistake.

"Don't come near me!" Tim yelled, and suddenly he sprang out of his chair and jumped out of the window. This was an impressive feat. The window wasn't even open.

I couldn't believe what had happened. I knew Tim was stupid but this was remarkable even by his standards. Maybe sleeping in a suit of armour had done something to that tiny organism he called his brain. At the same time, I was suddenly worried. I knew who the killer was now and I knew who was lined up to be the next victim. Tim was outside the house, on his own. He had made himself into a perfect target.

I had no choice. I went after him, jumping through the shattered window. I could see Tim a short distance away, running towards the tail of Crocodile Island. I had no idea where he was going. But nor of course did he. He was panicking – just trying to put as much distance between the two of us as he could. Not easy considering he was trapped on a small island.

"Tim!" I called.

He didn't stop. I ran after him, following the path as it began to climb steeply up towards the cliffs. This was where the island tapered to a point. I slowed down. Tim had already reached the far end. He had nowhere else to go.

The wind blew his hair around his head as he turned to face me. He was still holding the knife. I noticed now that it was a butter knife. If he stabbed me with all his strength he might just manage to give me a small bruise. His face was pale and his eyes were wide open and staring. The last time I had seen him like this was when they had shown *Jurassic Park* on TV.

"Get back, Nick!" he yelled. It was hard to hear him above the crash of the waves.

"You're crazy, Tim!" I called back. "Why would I want to hurt you? I'm your brother. Think about all the adventures we've had together! I've saved your life lots of times." I thought of telling him that I loved him but he'd have known that wasn't true. "I quite like you!" I said. "You've looked after me ever since Mum and Dad emigrated to Australia. We've had fun together!"

Tim hesitated. I could see the doubt in his eyes. He lowered the butter knife. A huge wave rolled in and crashed against the rocks, spraying us both with freezing, salt water. I looked past Tim at the rocks, an idea forming in my mind. There were six iron grey rocks, jutting out of the sea. I had noticed them the day we had searched the island. And of course, rocks like that have a name. Long and slender with pointed tops, standing upright in the water...

They're called needles.

I'm not exactly sure what happened next but I do know that it all happened at the same time.

There was a soft explosion, just where Tim was standing. The earth underneath his feet seemed to separate, falling away.

Tim screamed and his arm jerked. The butter knife spun in the air, the sun glinting off the blade.

I yelled out and threw myself forward. Somehow my hands managed to grab hold of Tim's shirt.

"Don't kill me!" Tim whimpered.

"I'm not killing you, you idiot!" I yelled. "I'm saving you!"

We rolled back together, away from the edge of the cliff ... an edge that was now several centimetres closer to us than it had been seconds before. I was dazed and there was grass in my mouth, but I realized that the killer had struck again. There had been a small explosive charge buried in the ground at the end of the cliff. Someone had detonated it and if I hadn't managed to grab hold of Tim, he would have fallen down towards to the sea, only to crash onto the needles fifty metres below.

We lay on the grass, panting. The sun was beating down on us. It was difficult to see. But then I became aware of a shadow moving towards us. I rolled over and looked up at the figure, limping towards us, a radio transmitter in one hand and a gun in the other.

"Well, well, well," he said. "It looks as if my little plan has finally come unstuck. And just when everything was going so well, too!"

Tim stared at the man. At his single eye,

his single leg, his huge beard. "It's … it's…" he began.

"It's Horatio Randle," I said. "Captain of the *Silver Medal,* the boat that brought us here."

"You got it in one, young lad!" he said.

"But that's not his real name," I went on. "Randle is an anagram. If you switch around the letters, you get…"

"Endral!" Tim exclaimed.

"Nadler," I said. "I think this must be Johnny Nadler. Your old school friend from St Egbert's."

The captain put down the radio transmitter. He had used it, of course, to set off the explosive charge a few moments before. He didn't let go of the gun. With his free hand, he reached up and pulled off the fake beard, the wig and the eye patch. At the same time, he twisted round and released the leg that he'd had tied up behind his back. It only took a few seconds but at once I recognized the thin-faced teenager I had seen in the photograph.

"It seems you've worked it all out," he muttered. His accent had changed too. He was no longer the jolly captain. He was a killer. And he was mad.

"Yes," I said.

"But it's impossible!" Tim burbled. "He couldn't have killed all the others. We looked! There was nobody else on the island!"

"It was Nadler all along," I said. I glanced

233

at him. The wind raced past and the waves crashed down.

He smiled. "Do go on," he snarled.

"I know what you did," I said. "Last Wednesday, you met us all at the quay, disguised as a captain. You'd sent everyone invitations to this reunion on the island and you even offered to pay a thousand pounds to make sure that they'd all come. Rory McDougal had nothing to do with it, of course. You'd killed him before we even set sail."

"That's right," Nadler said. He was smiling now. There was something horrible about that smile. He was sure this was one story I wouldn't be telling anyone else.

"You killed Rory and you left the poisoned chocolate for Sylvie. Then you dropped us on the island and sailed away again. There was no need for you to stay. Everything was already prepared."

"Are you saying … he wasn't here when he killed everyone?" Tim asked. He was still lying on the grass. There was a buttercup lodged behind his ear.

"That's right. Don't you remember what Mark told us when we were looking at the picture? He said that Johnny Nadler wanted to be an inventor when he left school. He said he was always playing with planes and cars." I glanced at the transmitter lying on the ground just a few feet away. "I assume they were radio-controlled planes and cars," I said.

"That's right!" Tim said. "He was brilliant, Nick! He once landed a helicopter on the science teacher's head!"

"Well, that's how he killed everyone on the island – after he'd finished with Rory McDougal and Sylvie Binns." I took a deep breath, wondering if there was anything I could do. Tim was right next to the edge of the cliff. I was a couple of metres in front of him. We were both lying down. Nadler was standing over us, aiming with the gun. If we so much as moved, he could shoot us both. I had to keep talking and hope that I might somehow find a way to distract him.

"Janet Rhodes was stabbed with an Eiffel Tower," I went on. "But I noticed that there was a tear in the canopy above her bed. I should have put two and two together and realized that the Eiffel Tower was always there, above the bed. It must have been mounted on some sort of spring mechanism. Nadler knew that was where she'd be sleeping. All he had to do was press a button and send the model plunging down. He was probably miles away when he killed her."

"That's right!" Nadler giggled. "I was back on the mainland. I was nowhere near!"

"But what about the face you saw?" Tim asked. "The skull at the window! Brenda saw it too!"

235

"You've already answered that one, Tim," I said. "A remote control helicopter or something with a mask hanging underneath. Nadler controlled that too. It was easy!"

"But how could he see us?"

I glanced at Nadler and he nodded. He was happy for me to explain how it had been done.

"The whole island is covered in cameras," I said. "That was Rory's security system. We've been watched from the moment we arrived. Nadler knew where we were every minute of the day."

"Right again!" Nadler grinned. He was pleased with himself, I could see that. "It was easy to hack into McDougal's security system and redirect the pictures to my own TV monitor. I was even able to watch you in the bath!"

"That's outrageous!" Tim was blushing. He knew that Nadler would have seen him playing with his plastic duck.

"Nadler had positioned the globe up on the roof," I went on. "If we'd gone up and looked we'd probably have found some sort of ramp with a simple switch. He waited until Libby Goldman came out of the front door and then he pressed the button that released the globe. It rolled forward and that was that. She never had a chance. He killed Eric and Brenda the same way. First he turned out the lights. Then he fired a bullet and brought down an organ pipe ... both by remote control." I paused.

"How about Mark Tyler?" I asked.

"The javelin was hidden in the branches of a tree," Nadler explained. "It was on a giant elastic band. Remote control again. It was just like a crossbow." He giggled for a second time. "Only bigger."

Well that explained the leaves. Some of them must have travelled with the javelin when it was fired.

"And that just left you, Tim," I said. "Nadler had to wait until you came out here. Then he was going to blow the ground out from beneath your feet and watch you fall onto the needles below. And with you dead, his revenge would be complete."

"Revenge?" Tim was genuinely puzzled. "But why did he want revenge? We never did anything to him!"

"I think it was because he came second," I said. I turned to Nadler. "You came second in every subject at school. And the boat you picked us up in. It was called the *Silver Medal*. I guess you chose the name on purpose. Because that's what you're given when you come second."

"That's right." Nadler nodded and now his face had darkened and his lips were twisted into an expression of pain. His finger tightened on the trigger and he looked at me with hatred in his eyes. "I came second in maths, second in chemistry, second in French, second in

237

geography, second in history, second in music and second in sport. I even came second in needlework, even though my embroidered tea towel was much more beautiful than your brother's stupid handkerchief!"

"It was a lovely handkerchief!" Tim said.

"Shut up!" Nadler screamed and for a moment I was afraid he was going to shoot Tim then and there. "Do you have any idea how horrible it is coming second?" he went on. Saliva flecked at his lips. The hand with the gun never moved. "Coming last doesn't matter. Coming fifth or sixth ... who cares? But when you come second, everyone knows. You've just missed! You've missed getting the prize by just a few marks. And everyone feels sorry for you. Poor old Johnny! He couldn't quite make it. He wasn't quite good enough."

He took a deep breath. "I've been coming second all my life. I go for jobs and I get down to the last two in the interviews but it's always the other person who gets it. I went out with a girl but then she decided to marry someone else because as far as she was concerned, I was Number Two. When I've tried to sell my inventions, I've discovered that someone else has always got there first. Number Two! Number Two! Number Two! I hate being Number Two...!

"And it's all your fault!" He pointed the gun at Tim and now the fury was back in his

238

eyes. "It all started at St Egbert's! That hateful school! That was where I started coming second and that was why I decided to have my revenge. You all thought you were clever beating me at everything. Well, I've showed you! I've killed the whole lot of you and I've done it in exactly the way you deserve!"

"You haven't killed me!" Tim exclaimed.

I didn't think it was a good idea to point this out. Nadler steadied the gun. "I'm going to do that now," he said. "Your body will still end up smashing into the needles so everything will have worked out the way it was meant to." He nodded at me. "I'll have to kill you too, of course," he continued. "You weren't meant to be here, but I don't mind. You sound too clever for your own good. I'm going to enjoy killing you too!"

He took aim.

"No!" I shouted.

He fired at Tim.

"Missed!" Tim laughed and rolled to one side. He was still laughing when he rolled over the side of the cliff.

"Tim!" I yelled.

"Now it's your turn," Nadler said.

I closed my eyes. There was nothing I could do.

There was a long pause. I opened them again.

Nadler was still standing, but even as I watched he crumpled to the ground. Eric

Draper, the fat solicitor, was standing behind him. There was blood all over his shirt and he was deathly pale. But he was still alive. He was holding the blunderbuss, which he must have taken from the bear. He hadn't fired it. He had used it like a club and knocked Nadler out.

"He only wounded me..." he gasped. "I woke up this morning. I came to find you..."

But I wasn't interested in Eric Draper, even if he had just saved my life. I crawled over to the cliff edge and looked down, expecting to see Tim, smashed to pieces, on the rocks below.

"Hello, Nick!" Tim said.

There was a gorse bush growing out of the side of the cliff. He had fallen right onto it. I held out a hand. Tim took it. I pulled him to safety and we both lay there in the sun, exhausted, glad to be alive.

We found the *Silver Medal* moored at the jetty and I steered it back towards the mainland. Eric was slumped on the deck. Johnny Nadler was down below, tied up with so much rope that only his head was showing. We weren't taking any chances after what had happened. We had already radioed ahead to the police. They would be waiting when we got to the mainland. Tim was standing next to me. We had left six dead bodies behind us on Crocodile

Island. Well, I warned you that it was going to be a horror story.

"I'm sorry I thought you were the killer," Tim said. He was looking even more sheepish than ... well, a sheep.

"It's all right, Tim," I said. "It's a mistake anyone could have made." He swayed on his feet and suddenly I felt sorry for him. "Do you want to sit down?" I asked. "It's going to take us a while to get back."

Tim shook his head. "No." He blushed. "I can't!"

"Why not?"

"That bush I fell into. It was very prickly. My bottom's full of..."

"What?"

"...needles!"

I pushed down on the throttle and the boat surged forward. Behind us, Crocodile Island shimmered in the morning mist until at last it had disappeared.

THE GREEK WHO STOLE CHRISTMAS

DEATH THREAT

I knew it was going to be a bad Christmas when I walked past the charity shop and the manager ran out and tried to offer me charity. It seemed that everyone in Camden Town knew I was broke. Even the turkeys were laughing at me. On the last day of term, the teachers had a whip-round for me … not that I really needed a whip, but I suppose it's the thought that counts. Christmas was just a few weeks away and the only money I had was a ten-pound book token that my parents had sent me from Australia. I tried to swap it for hard cash at my local bookshop, but the manager – a thin-faced woman in her forties – was completely heartless.

"I need to eat," I explained.

"Then buy a cookery book."

"I can't afford the ingredients!"

"I'm sorry. You can only use a book token to buy books."

"What's the point of buying books if I'm too faint to read?"

She smiled sadly at me. "Have you tried Philip Pullman?"

"No. Do you think he'd lend me some money?"

I couldn't believe my parents had sent me a book token for Christmas, but then of course they had no idea about anything. My dad had moved them to Sydney a few years before – he was a door-to-door salesman, selling doors, and he must have been doing well because this year he'd printed his own Christmas card. HAVE AN A-DOOR-ABLE CHRISTMAS, it said on the cover. There was a picture of a kangaroo with a red hat on, looking out of an open door. I was still laughing as I ripped it to pieces. My parents had two new kids of their own now: Doreen and Dora. Two sisters I'd never met. That made me sad sometimes. They weren't even two years old and they probably had more spare cash than me.

I was thinking about Australia as I walked home from the bookshop. My mum and dad had wanted to take me with them when they emigrated, and maybe it had been a mistake to slip off the plane before it took off. While it was taxiing down the runway, I was running away to find a taxi – and they hadn't even noticed until they were thirty-five thousand feet above France. Apparently my mum had hysterics. And my dad had my lunch.

I'm still not sure it was a smart decision. They say that London is like a village, and I certainly enjoyed living there. The only trouble was, I'd moved in with the village idiot. I'm talking, of course, about my big brother, Herbert Timothy Simple. But that wasn't what he called himself. He called himself Tim Diamond, Private Detective – and that's what it said in the Yellow Pages, along with the line: "No problem too problematic." He'd written that himself.

Tim was the worst private detective in England. I mean ... he'd just spent two weeks working in a big department store in the West End. He was supposed to be looking out for shoplifters but I don't think he'd kept his eye on the ball. In fact, the ball was the first thing that got stolen. After that, things went from bad to worse. The store had twenty-three departments when he started but only sixteen when he left. He was fired, of course. The dummies in the window probably had a higher IQ than Tim. He was lucky he had me. I solved the crimes, Tim got the credit. That was how it worked. If you've read my other stories, you'll know what I'm talking about. If you haven't, go out and buy the books. If you like, I'll even sell you a ten-quid book token. You can have it for nine quid.

Anyway, right now Tim was out of work. And November had arrived like a bad dog, snapping at everyone in the street and sending them hurrying home. As usual, it wasn't going to snow – but the pipes were frozen, the puddles had iced over and you could see people's breath in the air.

They were playing a Christmas carol on the radio as I let myself in. Tim was sitting at his desk wrapped in a blanket, trying to open a tin of sardines that was so far past its sell-by date he'd probably have more luck selling it as an antique.

I threw myself into a chair. "Any news?" I asked. "I don't suppose anyone has offered you a job?"

"I just don't get it," Tim replied. "You'd think someone, somewhere would need a private detective. Why is no one hiring me?"

"Maybe it's because you're no good," I said.

"You might be right," Tim nodded sadly.

"There are police dogs that have solved more crimes than you."

"Yes," Tim agreed, "but at least I don't have fleas."

I got up and turned the radio off. Tim had managed to get the tin open and the room was suddenly filled with the smell of twenty-seven-year-old sardines. And it was just then that there was a knock on the door.

I looked at Tim. Tim looked at me. We had

248

a client and we also had a room that looked like a rubbish tip and smelled like the River Thames during the Great Plague.

"One minute!" Tim shouted.

In that one minute, we raced around like two people in a speeded up commercial for Fairy Liquid. Papers went into drawers. Plates went into the kitchen. The sardines went into the bin and the bin went out the window. Sixty seconds later, the office looked more like an office and Tim was sitting behind his desk with a straightened tie and a crooked smile. I took one last look around and opened the door.

A man walked in. I guessed he was in his forties: short and fat, smoking a cigar. The cigar was short and fat too. He was dressed in a nasty suit. The pattern was so loud you could almost hear it coming. He had black, greasy hair, thick lips and eyes that would have been nicer if they'd matched. His shoes had been polished until you could see your face in them – though with his face I wouldn't have bothered. There was a gold signet ring on his finger. The way it squeezed the flesh, I doubted it would ever come off.

"You always keep your clients waiting outside?" he demanded as he came in and took a chair.

"We were filing," Tim explained.

He looked around. "I don't see no filing cabinets." He spoke like an American but he wasn't one. He was just someone who spent too much time on planes.

"We were filing our nails," I said.

He helped himself to one of Tim's business cards from the desk. "Are you Tim Diamond?"

"Yeah. That's me." Tim narrowed his eyes. He always does that when he's trying to look serious. Unfortunately it just makes him look short-sighted. "I'm a private eye."

"I know," the man growled. "That's why I'm here. My name is Jake Hammill and I want to hire you."

"You want to hire me?" Tim couldn't believe it. He leant forward. "So what can I do for you, Mr Camel?"

"Not Jay Camel. I'm Jake Hammill. You want me to spell it for you?"

"N-O," Tim said.

"I work in the music industry. As a matter of fact, I'm the manager of a woman who's a very famous pop singer."

Tim scowled. "If she's so famous, how come I've never heard of her?"

"I haven't told you her name yet."

"Maybe it would help if you did."

Hammill glanced at me. He was obviously suspicious. He turned back to Tim. "Can you keep a secret?" he asked.

"I'm not going to tell you," Tim replied.

"All right." Hammill nodded. "Her name is Minerva."

I have to admit, I was surprised. Hammill looked pretty small-time to me, but Minerva was one of the biggest names in the business. She was a multimillionaire pop singer and a movie actress. I doubted there was anyone in the world who hadn't seen her videos. She was the woman with the golden voice and the silver-plated breasts. Her clothes were outrageous – like the rest of her lifestyle. She had been born in Greece but now she lived most of the time in New York. The fact that she was visiting London had made the front page of every newspaper ... even the *Financial Times*.

"The thing is," Hammill said, "I've got a serious problem..." He twisted his signet ring nervously around his finger like he was trying to take it off. "Listen to me," he went on. "Minerva has been invited over here for Christmas. Tomorrow she's turning on the Christmas lights in Regent Street. And on Thursday at midday she's opening the Santa Claus grotto at Harrods department store in Knightsbridge. There's going to be a lot of press. A lot of TV. It's great publicity. But this is the problem..." He drew a breath. "I think she's in danger."

"What makes you think that?" I asked.

"Well, yesterday she received an anonymous letter."

"An anonymous letter!" Tim exclaimed. "Who from?"

Hammill scowled. "I don't know. It was anonymous. But it threatens her with death."

"So where is this letter, Mr Hubble?" Tim asked.

"It was sent to Minerva. She's got it. I'd like you to come and meet her at her hotel and she'll take you through it."

"She'll take me through the hotel?"

"No. She'll take you through the letter." He leant forward and already I could see the doubt in his face. "I have to say, Mr Diamond, I need to be sure you're the right man for this job. I wanted to go to the police, but Minerva's husband insisted that a private detective would be better. I understand you advertise in the Yellow Pages."

"Yeah," I muttered. "They match his teeth."

"I take it you know how to look after yourself," Hammill said.

Tim looked puzzled. "But I'm not ill!" he muttered.

Hammill rolled his eyes. Maybe I was imagining things but I could have sworn they went in opposite directions. "I'm not asking about your health," he said. "I need someone to stay close to Minerva while she's in London, and that may mean getting into a fight. So what I'm asking you is – do you know judo or karate?"

"Sure!" Tim nodded. "Judo, karate and

252

origami. When do you want me to start, Mr Rubble?"

It was obvious to me that Hammill was having second thoughts about Tim. And maybe third and fourth thoughts too. For a moment he bit his fingernail, deep in thought. Maybe he had plans to bite all the way down to the signet ring. Then he came to a decision. "All right," he said. "Minerva is staying at the Porchester hotel, which is in Hyde Park. That's highly confidential information by the way."

"What do you mean?" Tim demanded. "Everyone knows that the Porchester hotel is in Hyde Park."

"Sure. But nobody knows she's staying there. Otherwise we'd have fans all over the place."

"That would help with the ventilation…"

"Minerva likes her privacy. She's booked in under the name of Mrs Smith. Room sixteen. I want you to visit her this evening. Say, seven o'clock?"

"Seven o'clock," Tim said obediently.

"That's right. I'll let her take a look at you and if she thinks you're up to it, you're hired."

Tim nodded. I knew what was coming next. He was sitting back in his chair with his feet resting on his desk, trying to look every inch the private detective. The fact that he had a hole in one of his shoes didn't help. As far as he was concerned he was back in business.

And he was determined to prove it. "What about my fee?" he demanded.

"You're not hired yet," Hammill reminded him.

"OK, Mr Rabble. But I'd better let you know now, I'm not cheap. The only thing that goes cheap in this office is my budgerigar, and I don't think your superstar wants a bodyguard with feathers."

Hammill tried to make sense of this, decided it wasn't worth trying and stood up. "I'll see you this evening," he said. One last twist of the ring. It wasn't going anywhere, but he was. He walked out of the office, slamming the door behind him.

There was a moment's silence.

I went over to the cupboard and searched through the CDs. I knew we'd have a Minerva recording somewhere and, sure enough, there it was – her third album, *Think Pink*. I looked at the face on the cover: the blonde hair, the green eyes, the lips that looked like they could suck in a horse. Not for the first time I wished we had a CD player, but Tim had pawned it months ago. Along with just about everything else. That was another sad thought. When I walked into the Camden Town pawn shop, I felt more at home than I did at home.

But maybe our luck was going to change. All Tim had to do was protect her for a couple of days and there'd be a handsome cheque at the end of it. He might even end up taking a bullet for her. If so, I just hoped they'd pay him extra. And whatever happened, it might be fun to hang out with one of the biggest entertainers on the planet.

"I can't believe it!" I said. "We're going to meet Minerva!"

"It's even better than that," Tim replied. "She's opening the grotto at Harrods. Maybe we'll meet Father Christmas!"

I slid the CD back into the cupboard.

Minerva had just received a death threat and her husband had hired Tim Diamond. That was like getting her a knitted cardigan when what she really needed was a bullet-proof vest. Well, one thing was certain: this was going to be a Christmas to remember. I just wondered if Minerva would still be around to see in the New Year.

SUITE SIXTEEN

The Porchester was in the middle of London's Park Lane, a five-star hotel that cost the earth. The sort of place I wouldn't be able to stay in a blue moon. You could tell it was expensive: I spotted two celebrities in the revolving doors and by the time I'd reached the reception desk I'd passed three more. There was enough fur and jewellery in that place to fill a store. And that was just the men.

The reception area was all glass and marble, including the receptionist's dress. That's fashion for you. Tim and I had arrived half an hour early to drink in the atmosphere – and looking at the prices in the hotel bar we certainly weren't going to be drinking anything else. A glass of water here cost the same as a glass of wine anywhere else, and for a glass of wine you needed to take out a loan. Nothing cost peanuts here ... not even the peanuts.

That's the thing about the super-rich. They don't mind when things are crazily expensive. It just reminds them how rich they are.

We went over to the reception desk and asked to see "Mrs Smith". The receptionist was a slinky-looking girl with long fingernails. She had perfect teeth but she didn't smile and she spoke through her nose, so I guessed she didn't like showing them. She picked up a telephone and dialled a number with a fingernail that was a little longer than her finger. She spoke for a few seconds, then put the phone down. Her earrings jangled. So did my nerves.

"The second floor," she said, barely moving her lips. Maybe she was training to be a ventriloquist. "It's suite sixteen."

So Minerva had a suite, not a single room. We took the lift to the second floor and I have to admit I enjoyed the journey. It's the only lift I've ever seen with solid gold buttons and a chandelier. I could see Tim staring at everything as if he'd just died and gone to heaven. He'd insisted on putting on a suit, which he'd found at the bottom of the wardrobe. It was just a shame that the moths had found it first. Still, so long as nobody wondered why the jacket had seventeen buttonholes but only seven buttons, he'd be fine.

The lift door opened and we found ourselves in a corridor with about a mile of pink carpet, more chandeliers and the sort of wallpaper that seemed wasted on a wall. Suite sixteen was about halfway down – a double wooden door with gold numbers on.

Tim raised his hand, about to knock. And that was when we heard it. A sudden, loud crack from the other side. A gunshot? I wasn't so sure but Tim had no doubt at all. His eyes widened and he threw himself at the door – shoulder-first – obviously intending to smash it down, climb through the wreckage and rescue Minerva from whoever was taking pot shots at her. It didn't budge. Tim howled as he dislocated his shoulder. I reached out and opened the door. It was unlocked anyway.

We ran in. The door led straight into a plush living room. There were three people there. One of them was Jake Hammill, the manager who had come to our office that afternoon. The other was an older man dressed in a velvet jacket with a silk cravat around his neck. He had one of those permanent suntans that give your skin the colour of a peach but the texture of a prune. The third was Minerva. I recognized her at once with that strange buzz of excitement you get when you find yourself face to face with someone really famous. She was holding half a Christmas cracker. The tanned man was holding the other half. Well, that explained the bang we had just heard.

"Who the hell are you?" the older man asked.

"I'm Tim Diamond." Tim shrugged and I heard a loud click as his shoulder blade somehow managed to slip back into place. Well, that was something. Minerva looked as if she was about to call the police. At least she wouldn't have to ask for an ambulance too.

"So what do you mean just bursting in here?" the man continued. "Haven't you ever heard of knocking?"

"Wait a minute! Wait a minute!" Hammill interjected. "This is the private detective I was telling you about. The one you told me to see. Tim Diamond."

"What about the kid?" the man asked.

"I'm his little brother, Nick," I said.

"Yeah, well ... you'd better sit down."

Minerva had been watching all this with a mixture of puzzlement and disbelief. I sat down on the sofa next to her, thinking that a million kids would have given their right arm to be where I was right now and wondering what she'd do with a million right arms. She was dressed simply in expensive jeans and a white shirt, but even so she was one of the most beautiful women I'd ever seen. She had long, blonde hair, eyes that were somewhere between blue and green and the sort of body that made me wish I was older than fourteen. Maybe she was smaller than I'd imagined but then I don't have much imagination. And looking at her, I didn't need it. She was the real thing and she was right there next to me.

Meanwhile, Tim had sat down in a chair. I could tell he fancied Minerva too. As far as I know, Tim has never had a steady girlfriend. He just simply hasn't had any luck finding a woman who's attracted to a twenty-eight-year-old with no money and no brains. To be fair to Tim, he's not that unattractive. I mean, he's slim and he's dark and he's reasonably fit. And it seemed to me that Minerva was definitely interested in him. Mind you, if the old, wrinkled guy was her husband, I wasn't that surprised. How did a world-famous sex symbol end up married to her grandfather?

"So – how can I help you?" Tim asked with a lazy smile. He crossed one leg over the other and his foot caught a lamp, sending the shade flying.

"I told you," Hammill growled. "Minerva needs a bodyguard."

"With a body like that I'm not surprised!" Tim agreed.

"Hold on!" the old man interrupted. "That's my wife you're talking about."

"And who are you?" Tim asked.

"I'm her husband!" He was perched on the arm of the sofa next to Minerva. "My name is Harold Chase." He lay a hand on Minerva's shoulder, and maybe I was wrong but I could have sworn she shuddered slightly. "I'm paying you to make sure nobody hurts my baby."

"You've got a baby?" Tim demanded.

"I'm talking about Minerva!"

"I don't need looking after," Minerva said. They were the first words she had spoken, and I could hear the faint Greek accent fighting to get out. I was also reminded that this was the voice that had sold a billion CDs. "I don't need looking after"; it almost sounded like the title of one of her songs.

"We've got to take control of this situation," Hammill cut in. "You read what that letter said. Show it to Mr Diamond."

Minerva thought for a moment, then pulled a white envelope out of her pocket. She held it for a moment. "This arrived yesterday," she said. "It was slipped under the door of my suite. It's from somebody who hates me."

Tim opened the letter and read aloud:

"DEAR MINERVA, YOU ARE A MONSTER. I CANNOT FOREGIVE YOU FOR WHAT YOU DID IN TROPOJË LAST SUMMER. HOW COULD YOU DO THAT? I WILL NEVER FORGET IT AND VERY SOON I AM GOING TO KILL YOU. YOUR LIFE WILL COME TO AN END IN LONDON. THIS WILL BE YOUR LAST CHRISTMAS!"

261

Tim lowered the letter. "What makes you think that whoever wrote this hates you?" he asked.

Minerva stared at him. "I'm sorry?" she quavered.

"Well, he does call you *dear* Minerva…"

I snatched up the letter. It was straight out of a computer: blue ink on a plain sheet of paper. I noticed that whoever had written it couldn't spell "forgive". The envelope was addressed: Minerva, Suite 16.

"What happened in Tropojë?" I asked.

"Nothing happened in Tropojë," Harold replied.

"It's the concert," Hammill cut in. "It's gotta be!"

"Forget it, Jake."

"No, Harry. They might as well know." Hammill turned to us. "It was just one of those things," he explained. "It happened last summer, like the letter says. Minerva was going to give a big charity concert in Albania. It was to benefit OAK."

"What's OAK?"

"Overweight Albanian Kids. It tries to help kids who watch too much TV and eat too many McDonald's. Some of them have to wear elasticized clothing. Many of them are in wheelchairs. They can walk – they're just too lazy. Anyway, they were really looking forward to the concert, but at the last moment Minerva had to pull out."

"Why?" I asked.

"I had a headache," Minerva replied. Obviously the overweight kids of OAK had never given her much cause for concern. Until now.

"You upset a lot of fans, Minerva," Jake said.

"And you think one of the fans is out to get her?"

"That's what it looks like."

I wasn't so sure. The idea of an oversized Albanian TV addict travelling all the way to England to kill Minerva sounded a bit far-fetched to me. On the other hand, there was that spelling mistake: English clearly wasn't their first language. But there was something about the letter I didn't like – and I don't just mean the death threat. I knew there was something wrong. Something didn't add up. But I hadn't yet had time to work out what it was.

"My own feeling is that we should just get out of London," the husband said. "I can't sleep with the thought of you being in danger."

"Harold – you're exaggerating!" Minerva shook her head. "This trip is great publicity. Turning on the lights and opening the grotto is a big deal. I'm not going to run away just because some freak writes me a stupid letter." She turned to Tim. "I've got a single coming out on December twenty-fifth," she said.

"What's it called?" I asked.

Tim sighed. "It's called Christmas Day,

263

Nick," he said. "Everyone knows that."

"I mean – what's the single called?"

"It's a song about cowboys," Minerva said. "The title is 'Like a Virginian'." She fell silent for a moment and then she really surprised me. "If you boys are going to work with me, you might as well know that I hate this goddamn country and I hate Christmas."

"Minerva—" Harold began.

"Shut up, Harold! I just want to put my cards on the table."

"Your Christmas cards?" Tim asked.

"I don't have any. Those stupid pictures of angels and three wise men. If they were so wise, what was all that business with the gold, frankincense and myrrh? You think a baby's got any use for that sort of stuff?" She shook her head. "I hate everything about Christmas. Those stupid Christmas trees that drop needles all over the carpet. Those boring carols that go on and on. Santa Claus with his stupid beard."

"What about Christmas presents?" I asked.

"Why would I care about Christmas presents? I've got everything I want already." She realized she was still holding the half-cracker that she had pulled with her husband when we came in. "And I don't like these stupid crackers either," she went on. "They were sent up to the room by some fan or someone and all they've given me is a headache. As far as I'm concerned, the best thing to do with Christmas would be to forget the whole thing."

She threw down the cracker. A silver acorn and a slip of paper rolled out onto the table.

I don't know what it was that made me pick up the piece of paper. Maybe after Minerva's little speech I needed a laugh. Or maybe there was something about it that whispered to me that actually it didn't belong in a cracker. Anyway, I unfolded it and sure enough there was the same blue ink as the letter, the same typeface. There were just two lines.

WHEN MINERVA SEES THE LIGHTS
THAT'S WHEN I'LL HAVE HER IN MY SIGHTS

I read it out.

"I don't get it," Tim said. "It's not very funny…"

"It's not a joke, Tim!" I exclaimed. "It's another death threat."

"But that's impossible!" Harold seized the piece of paper and held it with a shaking hand. "How did this get inside the cracker?" he demanded. He stared at Jake Hammill. "You brought them up here!" he continued accusingly. "What's going on?"

"I just picked them up from reception!" Hammill replied. "They said they'd been left in your name by a fan."

"What does it mean?" Minerva asked. Her voice had gone quiet.

Nobody spoke – so I did. "It must mean tomorrow," I said. "When you turn on the Christmas lights." I picked up the acorn. It was heavy – solid silver, maybe. "And look at this," I said.

"An acorn…" Tim was puzzled.

"Off an *oak* tree, Tim," I said. "They're telling you who it came from."

"Of course!" Harold Chase stood up. He was shaking so much, I was worried something was going to fall off. "That's it," he said. "We're not going to turn on the lights. Forget it. We're not going anywhere near them."

"Harold…" Hammill began.

"I mean it, Jake."

"Forget it, Harold!" Minerva had also got to her feet. "Look – I've already promised. I'm going to turn on these stupid lights. I've got to be there: the Mayor of London is coming. All the press will be out. It's going to be a big event."

"It'll be an even bigger event if someone shoots you," I muttered.

Tim turned to me. "That's a terrible thing to say, Nick!" He thought for a moment. "Anyway, they might not shoot her. They might run her over or blow her up or possibly fix the wires so she gets electrocuted…"

Minerva had gone a little pale. "Do you think you can protect me, Mr Diamond?" she asked.

266

Tim smiled. "I'm the private eye who never blinks," he replied. "And from this moment I'm not going to let you out of my sight. I'm going to walk with you, eat with you and go to bed with you—"

"Hey! Wait a minute! I'm in the bed!" Harold interrupted.

"We have a four-poster," Minerva said.

"That's great," Tim said. "We can have one post each."

Jake Hammill stepped forward. "I think Minerva will be safe enough while she's here at the Porchester hotel," he said. "Suppose Mr Diamond joins us tomorrow evening on the way to Regent Street?"

Minerva nodded. "I'm staying in all day tomorrow. That'll be fine."

"That just leaves the question of your fee, Mr Diamond," Hammill continued.

"No question about it," Tim said. "I want one."

"Of course." Hammill blinked uncertainly. "We'll pay you two hundred pounds a day. But let's get one thing straight. If anyone takes a shot at Minerva, we'll expect you to step in front of the bullet."

"Don't worry!" Tim jerked a thumb at me. "That's what he's for."

So there it was, signed and sealed. I still wondered why Minerva hadn't gone straight to the police – but maybe it wouldn't suit

267

her being surrounded by the men in blue. I wanted to tell her that Tim would offer her about as much protection as a paper umbrella in the rain, but two hundred pounds was two hundred pounds. I watched as Jake Hammill counted out the money, and it occurred to me that the only time I'd been expecting to see the Queen that Christmas had been on her TV broadcast. But here were twenty little portraits sliding into Tim's outstretched hand. I almost wanted to kiss her. Or him.

We took the bus home. We could have afforded a cab but we'd already decided to blow a big chunk of the money on a three-course meal at our local Italian. I was already dreaming of a twelve-inch pizza on an eleven-inch plate. Extra cheese and pepperoni. And maybe extra pizza too. But even so, I couldn't get Minerva out of my mind. I went over what had happened in the suite. I was still certain something was wrong.

"If you ask me, Tim, there's something strange about this," I said.

Tim looked around him. "It's just a bus, Nick," he said.

"I'm not talking about the bus. I'm talking about Minerva. Those death threats! Whoever heard of a death threat inside a Christmas cracker?"

"Yeah," Tim nodded. "And there was no sign of a paper hat."

I shook my head. "I wouldn't be surprised if they weren't making the whole thing up ... the three of them. You heard what she said. All she wants to do is sell her CDs. Maybe the whole thing's just a publicity stunt."

Tim shook his head. "I don't think so, Nick. I think she's in real danger. Don't ask me why – I've just got an instinct for this sort of thing. A sixth sense."

"Sure," I muttered. "It's just a shame you missed out on the other five."

I looked out of the window. It had got dark a while ago and it looked as if it was going to snow. There were a few flakes dancing in the wind. As we turned a corner, I noticed a man standing on the pavement with a sandwich board. He was handing out leaflets about the end of the world. London is full of people like that. Maybe it's the city that drives them mad or maybe they're mad before they arrive and it's the city that attracts them. Anyway, this man had three words in red paint across his chest:

DEATH WILL COME

He seemed to catch my eye as we went past. And I found myself wondering. Was he just a harmless crank trying to sell religion to anyone who would listen?

Or did he know something I didn't?

REGENT STREET

Everyone makes a fuss about the Christmas lights on Regent Street and maybe there was a time when they were actually worth travelling in to see. I remember when I was small, my mum would take me into town and the lights would flicker and flash and sparkle and people would cross the road with their necks craned, staring at them in wonderment, and they wouldn't even complain when they were run over by the 139 bus.

But that was then. Nowadays the lights are more or less the same as they are on any other high street at Christmas. Worse than that, they're paid for by big business, so you don't just get Santa, stars or whatever. You get the latest characters from a Disney movie. Or "Harry Christmas" from J.K. Rowling. Or whatever.

Even so, turning on the lights is still a big

deal. If it isn't a member of the royal family, it's a pop star or a Hollywood actor. All the newspapers and TV stations record the moment when the button gets pressed, and the next day you can read all about it on page one: MINERVA LIGHTS UP LONDON. And just for one day the earthquakes and the wars and the dirty politics are left to page two.

We were driven to Regent Street in a stretch limo. The chauffeur was a tall, slim man in a grey uniform and I couldn't help wondering if someone hadn't stretched him too. Minerva and her husband sat on the back seat. For the first time I noticed he was wearing a hearing aid, but he didn't need it because no one was talking to him. She was gazing out of the window. It was made from special glass so that no one could look in. Her manager, Jake Hammill, had the next seat to himself. Tim and I were closest to the front – and furthest from the bar. The three of them were drinking champagne but all we'd been offered was a glass of iced water. Well, we were staff. Official security and its younger brother.

As usual Minerva was in a bad mood, but I had to admit that from where I was sitting she looked fabulous. She was wearing a bright red number with white fur trimmings. Think Father Christmas only thirty years younger and after major cosmetic surgery. Her lips were bright red too, shaped like a perfect kiss.

It would have been hard to believe that this was the woman who hated Christmas. She'd done herself up like the sort of present every man in London would want to open. I glanced at Tim and saw that he was drooling. I just hoped it wouldn't stain the carpet.

"Now, remember!" Harold Chase said to his wife. She turned round slowly and looked at him without a lot of interest. "You pose for the cameras. You make a little speech. You turn on the lights. And then we get the hell out of there."

"What's the big worry?" Minerva drawled.

"The big worry?" Harold's eyes bulged. For a nasty minute I thought they were going to fall out of his face. "There could be a killer out there, baby. You're going to be out in the open, exposed. Anyone could take a shot at you." He leant forward and turned to Tim. "You'd better keep your eyes open, Mr Diamond," he said.

"You don't have to worry, Mr Cheese," Tim assured him. "I've had my eyes on your wife all evening."

"Well, you'd just better make sure nothing goes wrong."

"What could possibly go wrong with me around?" Tim exclaimed. He threw his hands back in a gesture of surprise, emptying his glass of iced water over the driver.

The car drew to a halt. It was just coming up

to six o'clock on a cold, dry Tuesday evening, but the shops were still open and there were Christmas shoppers everywhere. We got out and suddenly the night seemed to explode in a thousand flashes. They came so thick and fast that I found myself blinded. It was as if I had entered an electrical storm that signalled the end of the world.

Of course, it was nothing so dramatic. Minerva was being photographed by a huge pack of press photographers, all of them holding up great, chunky cameras with lenses that were definitely pleased to see her. For a few seconds Minerva seemed to be frozen, half in the car and half out of it. Then she came to her senses and began to smile and wave; the silent, bad-tempered woman who had been sitting opposite me was instantly replaced by the perfect star that she was as the lights flashed all around her. And at that moment I got an idea of what it must be like to be a celebrity – loved not because of what you are but because of what the cameras want you to be.

At the same time, I was puzzled. Minerva had received two death threats. Even if she had decided not to take them seriously, her husband and manager had been worried enough to hire Tim and me. And yet here she was completely surrounded by photographers. It occurred to me that any one of them could have a gun. There were a few police around, but right now killing Minerva would be the easiest thing in the world. I said nothing. I could only stand there as she turned and smiled and smiled and turned while the photographers shouted at her from every side.

"Over here, Minerva!"

"Give us a smile, Minerva!"

"This way, Minerva!"

Tim nudged me. He was standing with his back to the car, blinking in the flashlights, but I could see that he was suddenly alert. I followed his eyes and saw a rather shabby-looking man in a suit hurrying towards us and suddenly I knew what was going to happen.

"Leave this to me..." Tim muttered.

"No, Tim!" I began.

But it was too late. Tim charged forward and grabbed hold of the man, then spun him around and threw him onto the bonnet of the limousine.

"That's far enough!" Tim exclaimed.

"I... I... I..." The man was too shocked to speak.

"What do you want with Minerva?" Tim demanded.

"I'm the Mayor of London!" the man exclaimed.

Tim looked suspicious. He was still pinning him down. "If you're the Mayor of London, where's your red cloak and pointy hat?"

"I'm not that sort of mayor," the man

growled. "I think you've been watching too many pantomimes."

"Oh no I haven't!" Tim replied.

By now, two policemen had appeared and had pulled Tim away, helping the Mayor to his feet. Because it *was* the Mayor, of course. I'd recognized him instantly – his bald head, his brightly coloured cheeks and his entirely colourless moustache. Jake Hammill had seen what had happened. He hurried over and placed himself between the Mayor and Tim.

"I'm so sorry!" he said. "We've hired private security and I guess he was a little jumpy."

"It's an outrage," the Mayor exclaimed. He had a whiny voice.

"Come and meet Minerva, Mr Mayor. She's been longing to say hello."

The thought of shaking Minerva's hand – or indeed any part of her – must have cheered the Mayor up because he seemed to have forgotten that he had just been attacked by Tim. Hammill took him over to his client, who was still posing for the cameras. "Minerva … this is the Mayor!" he said.

"How lovely to meet you, Mr Mayor!" Minerva sounded so genuine, I almost believed her myself. She kissed him on the cheek and night became day again as the photographers captured the moment for the morning's headlines. "Where do we go to turn on the lights?" she asked.

"This way…" The Mayor had gone red.

We made our way to a raised platform that had been constructed at the side of the road. There must have been four or five hundred people all around us, many of them waving autograph books and flashing cameras of their own. A Salvation Army band was playing carols. They finished "Away in a Manger" and began a version of "Silent Night" that was anything but.

Minerva climbed the stairs and I couldn't stop myself thinking of gallows and public hangings. I remembered the warning inside the cracker. Was someone really about to have a crack at her? I tried to think where I would hide myself if I were a sniper. I looked up at the rooftops. It was hard to see anything in the darkness but there didn't seem to be anyone there. How about an open window? All the windows in the street were closed. Then perhaps in the crowd…

By now Minerva had reached the top of the stairs. Was she being brave or stupid? Or was it just that she refused to take any of this seriously?

Jake Hammill was certainly looking nervous. So was Harold Chase. He was standing to one side, his hands in his pockets, pulling his black cashmere coat around him like he was trying to hide in it. His eyes were darting left and right. Even if nobody took a shot at his wife, I'd have said a major heart attack was a strong possibility. He didn't look like he'd last the night.

So there we all were on the platform: Minerva and the Mayor at the front, the rest of us grouped behind. There was a single red button, mounted on a wooden block, and a microphone. Minerva stepped forward. The crowd fell silent. The Salvation Army players came to the end of a verse and stopped – unfortunately not all at the same time.

"Ladies and gentlemen!" It was the Mayor speaking. His voice whined the full length of Regent Street and it wasn't just the fault of the microphone. "I'd like to welcome you all here and I hope you've all remembered to pay the congestion charge! We've had some great stars turn on the lights in Regent Street. But this year, if you ask me, we've got the biggest star of all. Please welcome … Minerva!"

Everyone clapped and cheered.

"Thank you. Thank you so very much!" Minerva's voice echoed after the Mayor's. "I'm so thrilled to be here, at Christmas. It's such a wonderful time of the year – the birth of baby Jesus and of course my new CD is about to be released. So Happy Christmas to everyone, and here goes…"

She lifted her finger.

And that was when it happened.

There were two gunshots. They sounded

incredibly close and there could be no doubt that Minerva was the target. At once the entire atmosphere changed. There was a single second of frozen silence and then screams as the crowd panicked and began to scatter, people pushing each other to get out of the way. The band was swept away in the stampede. I saw someone fall into the big drum. The cymbal player was knocked off her feet with a final crash. On the platform, the Mayor had been the first to dive for cover. Minerva hadn't moved, as if unsure what to do. I couldn't see if she had been hit or not. With that bright red dress, it was hard to tell.

Then Tim leapt into action. I have to hand it to him – at least he was braver than the Mayor, who had curled into a ball in the corner of the platform with his head buried in his hands. Tim had been hired to protect Minerva and that was what he was going to do – even if the shots had already been fired. Even if she was already dead.

"Get down!" he shouted.

He lunged forward and I guessed that he meant to throw himself on top of Minerva – which, I had to admit, was quite an attractive idea. Unfortunately, Minerva had already stepped aside. Tim missed and landed, with his arms outstretched, on the red button.

At once, ten thousand light bulbs burst into multi-coloured life. This year the Regent Street lights had been sponsored by McDonald's. They depicted stars and Christmas trees decorated with twinkling hamburgers and fries. At the same time, a specially arranged Christmas carol – "We Wish You a McMerry Christmas" – boomed out of the speakers.

The Mayor opened one eye. "You idiot!" he screamed. "You've turned on the Christmas lights instead of Minerva!"

I'm not sure what would have happened next. Perhaps Tim would have ended up being murdered himself. But then Harold Chase stepped forward and pointed. "There!" he yelled. "There he is!"

He was pointing at the rooftops and now, with all the extra bulbs burning below, the darkness had become a sea of red and blue and yellow and white. And sure enough, high above one of the department stores, I could make out a short, plump figure half hidden behind a chimney stack. He was staring down at us and, although I couldn't see what it was from this distance, there was definitely something in his hand. A gun? He certainly would have had a clear shot at Minerva from where he was standing – but not any more. Half a dozen policemen had already reached the platform and they had all grabbed a piece of her. Jake and Harold were also grabbing at her. Tim had crawled off the red button and was trying to climb on top. The entire platform looked like a training session for the All Blacks with Minerva in the middle of the scrum.

The figure on the roof didn't seem to be moving and that was when I decided to take action. I didn't really know what I was doing. Part of me was asking questions. Why hadn't I seen the sniper earlier? Why hadn't he made a faster escape – or at least tried to fire off a few more shots? Was that a gun in his hand? And part of me knew that I wouldn't find the answers hanging around on Regent Street. I had to go and look for them myself.

I leapt down from the platform, pushed my way through what was left of the crowd and plunged into the nearest shop. It was a huge place selling clothes that I couldn't possibly afford and – one glance told me – that I wouldn't want to buy if I could. Blue blazers and red cravats have never been my style. There was a lift opposite the front door and I was lucky. The doors were just closing as I arrived. I ran in and pressed the top button – the sixth floor. I was lucky again. The lift didn't stop on the way up.

The sixth floor seemed to be devoted to Christmas presents for people you don't like: really nasty golfing jumpers, oversized umbrellas and multicoloured shoes. There weren't too many shoppers around as I burst out of the lift and made for the nearest fire door. Sure enough, a flight of concrete stairs led up to the roof. I took them two at a time and it only occurred to me now that I was unarmed and about to come face to face with a would-be assassin who probably wouldn't be too pleased to see me. But it was too late to go back. And, I figured, he couldn't be more deadly than those golfing jumpers.

I reached a door marked FIRE EXIT and slammed into it … which, incidentally, set off all the fire alarms and the sprinkler system on the seven floors below. But now I was on the roof: a strange landscape of chimneys, satellite dishes, water tanks and air-conditioning units. I stopped for a moment and let my eyes get used to the darkness. Not that it was exactly pitch black. The Regent Street lights were still glittering below me and, looking down, I could see the scattered crowds, the police, what was left of the Salvation Army band.

Something moved. And there he was, the man that Harold Chase had seen from below. He was only about fifteen metres away from me, cowering on the other side of the roof. He didn't look like your typical assassin. He was short and very fat – almost spherical – with white, curly hair. I wondered if he was one of the overweight Albanians. It was Minerva's absence at a concert in Albania that had started all this.

The man looked at me with something between horror and dismay. He raised a hand as if to prevent me moving forward.

"No!" he shouted. "I d-d-didn't…"

Then he turned and ran.

I chased after him and that was when I discovered that I had miscalculated. I had run into the wrong store and there was a three-metre gap between his roof and mine. But I hadn't come this far to let an impossible jump and a probable fall to my death seven floors below worry me. I picked up speed and threw myself off the edge.

For a moment I hung in the air and I could feel the ground a very long way beneath me. The cold night air was rushing into me and – for a nasty moment – so was the pavement. The other roof was too far away. I wasn't going to make it. Suddenly I was angry with myself. Who did I think I was? Spider-Man? If so, I'd forgotten to pack a web.

But I didn't fall. Somehow my outstretched hands caught hold of the edge of the other roof and I winced as my stomach and shoulders slammed into the brickwork. I could taste blood and dust in my mouth. I'd cut my lip and maybe loosened a couple of my teeth. Using what little strength I had left, I managed to pull myself up and roll to safety. Painfully, I got to my feet. I wasn't surprised to see that the little fat man had gone.

He had left something behind. I saw them – three small silver objects on the asphalt. At first I thought they were bullets, but as I walked towards them, I realized they were too big. People down in the street were pointing up at me and shouting as I dropped to one knee and scooped them into my hand.

Three oak leaves. That was what the sniper had left behind. The acorn in the cracker and now this. He was definitely trying to tell me something and I'd got the message loud and clear.

DINNER FOR TWO

When I woke up the next morning, we were right back where we'd started. Which is to say, we were in Camden Town, in the office, and once again Tim was out of work. It turned out that nobody had been particularly impressed by my death-defying leap when all I'd got to show for it was grazed arms, bruises and a handful of silver oak leaves. I'd given the police a description of the man I'd seen on the roof – not that it added up to much. Small and fat. The curly hair could have been a wig. And although he had spoken, he hadn't said enough for me to be sure whether he had an Albanian accent or not.

As I'd sat in the bath that night, I'd gone over his words a dozen times. *No! I d-d-didn't...* Had he been scared or did he always stammer like that? And what had he meant? The police had decided that he was angry – that he was telling me he hadn't shot Minerva in the sense that he had missed. To me it seemed simpler than that. "I didn't do it. It wasn't me." That was what he had been trying to say. But then why had he left the oak leaves behind? Maybe they were the symbol of the society for Overweight Albanian Kids. And finally, where was the gun? I thought I'd seen something in his hand but he hadn't had it when I reached the roof.

Anyway, the case was over as far as we were concerned. Now that the police knew Minerva was in real danger, they had taken over protection duties – and looking at some of those officers leering at her on Regent Street, I could see that plenty of them were going to be putting in for overtime. The good news was that we still had about seventy pounds of the two hundred Jake Hammill had given us. That would buy us a Christmas turkey, Brussels sprouts, roast potatoes and chestnut stuffing. It was just a shame that Tim had sold the oven.

I found him at breakfast with a bowl of cornflakes and the morning newspaper. He wasn't looking too pleased and I soon saw why. He'd made the front page. There was a picture of him spread out on his stomach just after he had accidentally turned on the Christmas lights.

"Have you seen this?" he wailed as I sat down. "And look at this!"

He tapped the caption underneath the picture:

DIM DIAMOND ASSAULTS MAYOR AND TURNS ON THE LIGHTS

"It must be a misprint," he said.

"Are you sure?" I asked.

Tim sighed – and suddenly he was looking sad. "You know, Nick," he began. "Recently, I've been thinking."

"Did it hurt?" I muttered.

He ignored me. "Maybe I should think about getting another job. I mean, look at me! I'm twenty-eight. I never have any money. I'm six months behind on the rent. I can't remember the last time you and I had a square meal."

"We had pizza the night before last," I reminded him.

"That was circular. And whenever I do get a job – like this business with Miranda – it always seems to go wrong." He sighed again. "She told me I was the most stupid person she'd ever met."

"Maybe she was joking."

"She spat at me and tried to strangle me!"

"Well ... she's Greek."

Tim shook his head. "As soon as the New Year begins, I'm going to find myself a proper job," he said. "It shouldn't be too difficult. I've got qualifications."

I fell silent. I didn't have the heart to remind

him that he only had two A levels – and one of them was in embroidery.

It looked as if we were going to have a pretty glum Christmas. But as you'll probably know by now, nothing in our lives ever turns out quite how we expect. A second later there was a knock at the door and before either of us could react, Minerva walked in. I was so surprised, I almost fell off my chair. Tim was so surprised he actually did fall off his.

She was on her own and she was trying to look inconspicuous dressed in jeans and a black jersey with a one-thousand-dollar pair of sunglasses hiding her eyes. But Minerva was Minerva. She couldn't look inconspicuous if she covered herself in mud and sat in a swamp.

"Minerva!" Tim gasped as he picked himself up.

"I didn't want to see you," Minerva said, taking off her sunglasses so she could see him better. "I didn't want to come here," she went on. "But I had to. Last night I behaved like a cow."

"You ate grass?" Tim asked.

"No. I behaved disgracefully towards you. I spat at you. I tried to strangle you. But this morning, when I woke up, I realized I'd got it all wrong." She sat down. "Harold brought in the newspapers and I saw that we got every single front page. And part of that was thanks to you. *The Times* called you a maniac. The

Mail said you were idiotic. The *Guardian* thought you were a banker."

"That *was* a misprint," I said.

Minerva ignored me. "If I'd just turned on those ridiculous lights, the most I would have got would have been the front page of the evening paper. But the way things turned out, I got more publicity than I could have dreamed of. Harold is certain my new CD is going to go straight to number one."

"How is Harold?" I asked.

"He had a very lucky escape last night," Minerva said. "One of those bullets missed him by a centimetre. It even burnt a hole in the side of his coat."

"You mean … it could have hit his pacemaker?" I exclaimed.

"It was a near miss. But I'm not here to talk about Harold." She turned to Tim. "I want to make it up to you, Timothy," she said. "I want to invite you to dinner. I've already reserved a table for two."

"Isn't two a little early for dinner?" Tim asked.

"For just the two of us, I mean!" Minerva smiled but I wasn't entirely convinced. I'd met sharks with friendlier teeth. "At eight o'clock this evening," she went on. "There's a restaurant I go to. It's called The Gravy." She giggled mischievously. "I thought we might have a little tête-à-tête."

"I'm not that crazy about French food," Tim muttered.

"You'll like this," Minerva simpered. "Make sure you dress up smart. You should put on that suit of yours with seven buttons and seventeen buttonholes."

And with that she was gone.

I went over to the window and looked out as she left the building. There was a police car waiting for her. It was true, then. The men in blue had now taken over Tim's job.

"They're giving her round-the-clock protection," I said.

"They think someone's going to kill her near a clock?"

Tim looked slightly dazed. I could see that he was already imagining himself in some swanky restaurant, drinking champagne with the rich and famous. It was time to bring him down to earth.

"You're not going," I said.

"Why not?" Tim replied.

"She's not interested in you, Tim. If she's invited you out, it's only for the publicity. That's all she cares about."

"Maybe she's got a soft spot for me."

"I don't think she's got a soft spot for anyone except herself. Anyway, she's a married woman."

"Listen, kid." Tim leant back in his chair. "You don't understand the female mind.

Maybe she's looking for something rough and a little bit dangerous."

"Then she can buy herself a yak."

"She likes me!"

"She's using you, Tim."

"She's invited me to dinner!"

"Well, if you're going, I'm going too."

Tim stared at me as if I'd just slapped him in the face – and I can't say I wasn't tempted. "Forget it, Nick," he said. "You heard what she said. This is a dinner for two. I don't need you there. I'm going on my own. And this time, my decision is final!"

The Gravy was one of London's most exclusive restaurants, reserved for celebrities and millionaires. It was so exclusive, even the waiters had trouble getting in, and the name was written in tiny letters as if it didn't want anyone to notice. It was tucked away in a quiet street near Covent Garden with a doorman sizing up everyone who came close. He looked at Tim and me with an expression of complete disgust. But this was the sort of place where even the doormat didn't say WELCOME. It preferred to say GO AWAY.

Why had I come? Part of the answer was that I was worried about Tim. I still didn't know what Minerva was up to, but I didn't trust her and I wanted to be there if things took a turn for the worse. But also, I quite fancied dinner at The Gravy. The food was said to be so good that the chef actually cried when you ate it. The house speciality was a leg of lamb cooked in Armagnac – and no matter that it cost you an Armagnac and a leg. Even a glass of water at The Gravy was expensive. It probably came out of a gold-plated tap.

The head waiter showed us to the best table, and there was Minerva looking stunning in a white silk dress that hugged her tight in all the right places and tighter still in some of the wrong ones. Her face fell when she saw me but she didn't protest as a couple of waiters hastily added a third setting to the table. It was only as we sat down that she muttered, "I'm surprised you brought your little brother, Timothy. Couldn't you find a babysitter?"

"I'm no baby, Minerva," I said.

"I was hoping to be alone with your big brother. I want to get to know him a little better."

"Just pretend I'm not here."

And that's exactly what she tried to do for the rest of the meal. The waiter came over with three menus but she chose only for the two of them, leaving me to decide for myself. That suited me. I went for the straightforward steak and chips, leaving the fancy stuff with the French names to her and Tim. If I've got one rule in life, it's never eat anything you can't translate.

"So tell me, Timothy," Minerva said, winking at him. "How would you like a little bubbly?"

Tim looked awkward. "Actually, I had a bath before I came."

"Bollinger!" she exclaimed.

"No. Really. I did!"

Minerva ordered a bottle of Bollinger. I asked for a Coke. The way she was making eyes at Tim, it really did seem that she had designs on him and I couldn't understand it. I mean, he was fifteen years younger than her and about fifty thousand times poorer. What could she see in him? I watched him as he opened the champagne for her. There was an explosive pop, followed by a scream from the other side of the room.

"The head waiter?" Tim asked.

"No," I said. "Just a waiter's head."

Minerva didn't seem to mind. She snuggled up close to him. "I love a man who makes me laugh," she said. "Can I ask you something, Timothy? Do you have a girlfriend?"

"Not at the moment," Tim answered.

"There's nobody waiting for you in bed tonight?"

"It's just Tim and his Paddington Bear hot-water bottle," I told her.

Tim glared at me.

"I fill it for him every night."

The waiter arrived with the first course:

soup for me, caviar for Tim and Minerva. Personally, I've never understood caviar. I mean, when I order eggs, I don't expect them to turn up tiny, black and fifty quid a mouthful. But she seemed happy enough. I wondered who would pick up the bill.

I could see that Tim was already well out of his depth. He was looking more and more uncomfortable the closer Minerva got, and she was already close enough. Any closer and she would be on his lap.

"Timothy ... I think you and I were meant for each other," she breathed.

"What about your husband?" Tim squeaked.

She sniffed. "Let's not talk about Harold. He's half the man you are."

"Which half are you talking about?"

I couldn't help chipping in again. "If you dislike him so much," I asked, "why did you marry him?"

To my surprise, Minerva looked me in the eye for the first time and I knew at once that she was going to be completely honest. "Why do you think?" she replied coldly. "I married Harold for his money. That was at the start of my career. I'd just left Athens and I had nothing. He promised to help me – and he did. Of course, all that's changed now. Now I'm worth millions!"

"So why are you still with him?"

"I can't be bothered to divorce him. Anyway, it's more fun the way things are."

"Does he know where you are tonight?"

Minerva laughed. "Of course he knows. You should have seen his face when I told him I was going out with Timothy. I thought he was going to have a heart attack!"

So that was why she had invited Tim to The Gravy. I should have seen it from the start. Minerva loathed her husband – that much had been obvious when we first met them at their suite at the hotel – and she amused herself by humiliating him. And what better way than to be seen out in public with someone like my big brother, Tim?

At that moment I disliked her as much as anyone I had ever known. More than Charon, the four-fingered assassin we met in Amsterdam. More than my homicidal French teacher, Monsieur Palis. The thing about Minerva was that she was beautiful, rich and loved by millions. But she had the heart of a snake.

Somehow we got through to the next course. My steak was fine but I didn't like the look of the grey, jelly-like dish that Minerva had ordered for herself and Tim. It came in a yellow sauce with rice and beans.

Tim wasn't sure either. He had eaten about half of it when he stopped and looked up. "What did you say this was?" he asked.

"Cervelles de veaux au beurre."

He took another mouthful. "It tastes interesting," he said. "What does that mean?"

"Grilled calves' brains in butter."

Two minutes later we were standing outside on the pavement with the doorman glowering at us, glad to see us go.

"That was a nice evening," I said.

"Do you think Minerva enjoyed it?" Tim asked.

"Well, you may have spoiled it a bit when you were sick on her." I looked around for a bus or a taxi.

"I want to go home," Tim groaned. He was still looking very green.

"To Paddington Bear?"

"Just get us a cab!"

But as it turned out, we weren't going to need a bus or a cab. Because just then a car came screeching to a halt in front of us and two men leapt out.

"It's a police car!" Tim exclaimed.

That was particularly brilliant of him and I wasn't sure how he'd worked it out. Maybe it was the blue uniforms the men were wearing. Or it could have been the car with its flashing lights and the word POLICE emblazoned on the side. But he was right. I thought they'd come to look after Minerva – but it was the two of us they made for.

"Are you Tim Diamond?" one of them asked.

"Yes…"

"Get in the car. You're coming down to the station."

"What's going on?" I demanded. "What's happened? And how did you know we were here?"

They ignored me.

The policeman was examining Tim. "We want to talk to you," he said.

"What about?" Tim quavered.

The policeman smiled but without a shred of warmth or humour. It was the sort of smile a doctor might give you before he explained you only had a week to live. "You're wanted, Mr Diamond," he said. "For murder."

THE DEAD MAN

I don't like police stations. They're full of violent and dangerous characters who need to be kept away from modern society … and I'm not talking about the crooks. A lot of people say the British police are wonderful, but I'd have to disagree. I was only fourteen but I had been arrested so often, it couldn't be long before they gave me my own set of personalized handcuffs. I even spent a month in prison once – and I hadn't done anything wrong! When I look back on it, there's only one word to describe the way I've been treated. Criminal.

This time they drove us to a police station in Holborn, about ten minutes' drive from The Gravy. Tim had gone very pale and quiet in the back of the car. *Cervelles de veaux au beurre* and now this! We stopped and the two policemen led us in through a door and down the usual corridor with white tiles on the walls and hard neon lighting above … the sort of corridor that can only take you somewhere you don't want to be. There was an interrogation room at the end: four chairs, one table and two detectives. The furniture was hard and unattractive but that was nothing compared to the men.

Detective Chief Inspector Snape and Detective Superintendent Boyle. They were old friends and, like most of Tim's old friends, they hated us. Why was it that whenever we got into trouble, the two of them always seemed to show up? Surely the Metropolitan Police could have found two new officers to molest us? Anyway, put an ape and a Rottweiler in suits and you'll get a rough idea of Snape and Boyle. Snape was the older of the two and the one less likely to have rabies. He was looking old, I thought. But he'd probably looked old the day he was born.

"Well, this really is the perfect end to a horrible day," Snape began as we sat down. It didn't look as if he was going to offer us a cup of tea. "Tim Diamond! The only detective in London with no brains."

Tim went a little green.

"I wouldn't mention brains unless you know a good dry cleaner," I said.

"I want to go to bed!" Tim moaned.

"You're not going anywhere, Diamond," Snape cut in. "I'm investigating a murder and right now you're my only suspect."

"Can I hit him?" Boyle asked hopefully.

"No, Boyle."

"Can I hit his little brother?"

"No!"

"But they were resisting arrest, sir!"

"We haven't arrested them yet, Boyle." Snape shook his head and sighed. "I've just sent Boyle on an anger-management course," he told us.

"Did it work?" I asked.

"No. He got angry and hit the manager so they sent him back again."

"Well you're wasting your time," I said. "We haven't murdered anyone."

Snape looked at me with disdain. "What can you tell me about a man called Reginald Parker?" he said.

"I can't tell you anything, Snape," I said. "We've never met him."

"What's happened to him?" Tim asked.

"He's been murdered," Snape replied. "He was strangled this afternoon. He lived at 27 Sparrow Lane and his neighbour heard the sound of a fight. She called us and we found the body."

"What makes you think it's got anything to do with us?" I asked.

Snape nodded at Boyle. "Show them!"

Boyle leant down and produced a car battery connected to a tangle of wires with clamps on the end. He placed it on the table and glanced unpleasantly at Tim. Snape raised his eyes. "I don't mean that! I want you to show them the evidence!"

Boyle scowled. He opened a drawer and this time he produced a transparent evidence bag with something inside it. I recognized it at once. *No problem too problematic*. It was Tim's business card.

"We found this next to the body," Snape said. "How do you explain that?"

"A coincidence?" Tim suggested.

Snape's face darkened. "Of course it's not a coincidence, you idiot! It's a clue! Was Reginald Parker a client of yours? That wouldn't surprise me. Anyone stupid enough to hire you would almost certainly wind up dead."

I shook my head. "I told you, Chief Inspector. We've never seen him."

"How can you be so sure of that? I haven't even told you what he looked like."

Boyle opened the drawer a second time and produced a black and white photograph.

You can always tell when the police have taken a picture of someone after they're dead. They don't smile for the camera. In fact, they don't do anything. And the black and the white somehow seems to suit them. All the colour has already gone. The photograph showed a short, plump man with curly hair, lying on his back in the mess that had once been the room where he lived. I gasped. Because the truth was that I did know him. I had seen him once and only briefly, but it wasn't a face I was going to forget.

Reginald Parker was the man who had tried to shoot Minerva. He was the man on the roof above Regent Street.

"Did you find a gun in his room?" I asked.

Snape shook his head. "No. I told you. He was strangled."

"How about a handful of silver acorns? Or anything to do with oak trees?"

Boyle leant over the table and grabbed me by the collar. I felt myself being dragged to my feet. My feet left the floor. One of my shirt buttons went shooting over my shoulder. "Are you taking the mickey?" he demanded.

"No!" I gurgled. "I'm trying to help you. I did meet this man. I just didn't know his name."

Boyle turned to Snape, still holding me in the air. "Shall I wire him up to the car battery, sir?"

"Certainly not, Boyle!" Snape looked offended. "He's going to tell us everything anyway."

"I know that, sir. But this way he'll tell us quicker."

"Just put him down!"

Boyle looked on the edge of tears but he dropped me back into my seat. And then I

301

told them everything that had happened since Jake Hammill had walked into our office. The meeting at the hotel. The events in Regent Street. Snape nodded when I talked about that. He must have seen Tim on the news.

"You're sure it was Parker on the roof?" he asked.

"It's the same face, Chief Inspector," I said.

"And you think he was a member of this organization – Overweight Albanian Kids?"

"He was certainly overweight." I nodded at the photograph.

"But as far as we know, he wasn't Albanian."

"Maybe he lived in Albania when he was young."

"We'll check it out."

"Does this mean you're letting us go?" Tim asked, getting to his feet.

"Not so fast, Diamond!"

"All right." Tim sat down, then got up more slowly.

Snape glowered. "I'll see you two again!" he said.

"Yeah. And I'll be waiting." Boyle was standing there holding one of the electrical contacts in his hand. The other was on the table. I passed it to him.

"Don't forget this," I said.

He took it in the other hand.

We could still hear Boyle screaming as we raced back down the corridor and out onto the street. But that's the modern police for you. Shocking.

When Tim and I had breakfast the next morning, I could see he was deep in thought. He didn't even react when he upturned the cereal packet and got the plastic toy.

"I just don't get it," he said at length.

"What's that, Tim?"

"Well … this guy … Archibald Porter."

"I think you mean Reginald Parker."

"He tried to kill Minerva and now somebody has killed him. But that doesn't make any sense. Nobody knew who he was. So why kill him? If they wanted to protect Minerva, they could have just reported him to the police."

He frowned but then his eyes brightened. "Maybe it was just another coincidence!" he exclaimed. "Maybe his death was an accident!"

"It's quite tricky to get strangled by accident," I pointed out.

Tim nodded. "I wonder how he got my business card?"

"That's exactly what we're going to find out…"

We were lucky that Snape had given us Parker's address. As soon as Tim had finished breakfast, we looked up Sparrow Lane in Tim's A–Z. Actually, it was an A–W. He'd got it cheap. Then we took a bus to the other side of

London and a narrow street of terraced houses not far from the old meat market. Number 27 was halfway down and looked exactly the same as numbers 25 and 29 – apart, that is, from the policeman on duty and the blue and white POLICE LINE: DO NOT CROSS taped over the front door.

To be honest, I'd forgotten that Snape would have left someone on duty and I could see at a glance that we weren't going to get past the policeman at the door. He had the sort of face that if he ever decided to join the dog unit, he wouldn't need a dog. Ignoring him, I went straight to the house next door and rang the bell, hoping the owner would be in.

She was. The door opened and a huge, cheerful Caribbean woman in a brilliantly coloured dress appeared on the doorstep, the great slabs that were arms folded across her ample breast. "Yes, me darlings? How can I help you?" she boomed out.

I nudged Tim.

"I'm Tim Diamond," Tim said.

"Yes?" The woman was none the wiser.

"My brother is a private detective," I told her. "He wants to ask you some questions about the guy who lived next door."

"That's right," Tim explained. "And if he lived next door, then I'd imagine he must have been your neighbour."

"That's brilliant, Tim," I muttered. "How did you work that one out?"

It turned out that the woman was called Mrs Winterbotham and had lived at number 25 for almost as many years. Her husband was out, working at the meat market, and she invited us into her kitchen and gave us tea and coconut biscuits. She had already told the police everything but she was going to enjoy telling us again.

"Reginald was an actor," she said, then looked left and right and lowered her voice as if he might be listening from beyond the grave. "But he wasn't a very good one. Oh no! He was out of work most of the time. He was in *The Cherry Orchard* last May, playing one of the cherries. And last year he appeared at the Unicorn Theatre in a one-man show."

"Was it popular?" I asked.

"No. Only one man came." Mrs Winterbotham dropped three sugar cubes into her tea and helped herself to another biscuit. "Reginald was a nice man. But, you know, I'm not sure it really helped his career, his having a stutter."

I remembered now. Parker had stuttered when he was on the roof. So it hadn't been because he was afraid.

"I said to him that he ought to be a mime artist," Mrs Winterbotham went on. "That way he wouldn't have had to talk. But I don't think people would have paid to see him. He didn't have the figure for it. To be honest with you, I've seen more attractive figures hanging up in the meat market."

"When was his last job?" I asked.

"Well…" She put down the biscuit and leant forward conspiratorially. "That's what I told the police. He always got a job at Christmas. He worked in a department store. But this year something very unusual happened. He got paid for a one-night appearance in the West End! He didn't tell me what it was but I do know that it was a lot of money."

"Who paid him?"

"He never said. But I don't think it can have worked out because when I saw him the next morning, he was very upset."

"How do you know he was upset?" Tim asked.

"He was crying."

"You're sure they weren't tears of happiness?"

"Oh no, Mr Diamond. He was completely miserable. And then that afternoon, someone came to the house. I heard this banging and crashing and I went round to the garden to see what was happening. Then there was silence. I knocked on the door but I got no answer. So I called the police."

"Just one last question, Mrs Winterbotham…" I began.

"Please. Call me Janey!"

"Was Reginald Parker Albanian?"

"No. As far as I know, he'd never been to Albania. In fact, he never went anywhere. He couldn't afford it. Most of the time he just sat at home and watched TV." She sighed and I got the idea that maybe she'd been his only friend in the world. "And now he's dead. I can't believe it. Now, how about a nice piece of banana cake?"

We didn't have the cake.

Because suddenly, even as Mrs Winterbotham had been talking, everything had made sense. Suddenly I was back on the roof, hearing Reginald Parker as he called out across the gap. *I d-d-didn't...* I saw the cracker with the acorn and the death threat and knew what it was that was wrong with the letter Minerva had been sent. I thought about Regent Street and the bullet that had come so close it had drilled a hole in Harold Chase's coat. I knew exactly what job Reginald had been hired for – it could only be one job – and I also knew what was going to happen at twelve o'clock that day. I looked at my watch. It was five past eleven. We had less than one hour left.

"We have to get to Harrods, Tim!" I said.

Tim shook his head. "This is no time for Christmas shopping, Nick."

"We're not going shopping. We have to find Minerva."

"Why?"

A taxi drove by. I reached out and flagged it down.

"She's going to be murdered, Tim. And I know who by."

KILLER WITH A SMILE

We were on the wrong side of town. We had to cross the whole of London to reach Knightsbridge, and with Christmas just weeks away the traffic could hardly be worse. As we sat in a traffic jam on the edge of Hyde Park I could feel the minutes ticking away. Worse than that, I could see them. The taxi meter was running and Tim was staring at it in dismay, watching as the last of his earnings disappeared.

We finally made it with about five minutes and ten pounds to spare, but even so it was going to be tight. Harrods was a huge place and the grotto was right up on the fourth floor. Worse than that, the entire store was heaving – not just with shoppers but with the usual crowd of fans and policemen who had turned out to see or to protect Minerva. There were security men on all the doors and more photographers waiting in the street, although you'd have thought by now the papers would have had enough of her. I certainly had.

And what nobody knew was that the killer was already inside the building. He would smile at Minerva and he would murder her ... and she wouldn't even know it had happened until she woke up dead.

"This way, Tim!"

We had plunged off the street and into women's handbags, then into cosmetics, then food. Harrods was every Christmas present you could ever imagine – more presents than anyone in the world could ever want. It was Christmas gone mad: hundreds of miles of tinsel; thousands of glittering stars and balls; enough Christmas trees to repopulate a forest. Don't get me wrong. I love Christmas and I'll tear open as many presents as I can get my hands on. But as I ran for the escalators, past the groaning shelves and the grinning sales assistants, I couldn't help but feel there had to be something more to it than this. Maybe something less, if you know what I mean.

We reached the escalators and began to fight our way up. I had a strange sense of déjà vu as I went. Suddenly I was in another department store in a different part of London almost two years before. I'd been running then too – to escape from two German assassins who'd been trying to make sure that the only way I saw Boxing Day was from inside a box. But that was another time and another story and if you want to know about it, I'm afraid you're going to have to buy another book.

We got to the fourth floor and there was a sign pointing towards Santa's grotto, "Jingle Bells" blaring out of the speakers and little kids everywhere, dragging their mothers to see the man in red.

I stopped, panting. "I hope we're not too late," I gasped.

"Yes," Tim agreed. "Santa may not have any presents left!"

Sometimes I think Tim doesn't belong in the real world. Maybe he'd be more comfortable in a nice white room with padded walls. But this was no time to argue. It was twelve noon exactly. Somewhere in the clock department down below, a thousand clocks would be chiming, bleeping or shooting out cuckoos. The grotto had just been opened by Minerva. And the way ahead was blocked.

There were toys everywhere. Vast Lego castles, cuddly toys, jigsaw mountains and Scalextric cars buzzing round in furious circles. Children were pulling and pushing in every direction. In the far distance I could see the green, plastic entrance to a green, plastic cave with a long line of people waiting to go in. That was where we had to be. But our path had been closed off by a sixteen-stone store security guard with the body of a wrestler and the face of a boxer at the end of a particularly vicious fight. At least, I assumed he was a security guard. It was hard to be sure. He was dressed as an elf.

"You can't go this way!" he told me. "You have to go to the back of the queue." So he *was* a security guard. I should have known. How many elves do you see carrying truncheons?

"Where's Minerva?" I demanded. I was afraid I was already too late – and this brute in green tights was only making things worse.

"She's in with Santa Claus, opening the grotto. You'll have to wait in line if you want her autograph."

"I don't want her autograph. I want to save her life!"

But it was no good. I might as well have argued with Rudolph the Red-Nosed Reindeer (there was a mechanical version next to the cave). I had to stop myself pulling out my hair. I was expecting a gunshot at any moment and here I was trying to reason with an elf. I looked around me, wondering if I could bribe him with a cuddly toy – or if not, hit him with one. That was when I saw Detective Chief Inspector Snape, standing grim-faced with Boyle next to him, the two of them surrounded by Barbie dolls.

"Snape!" I shouted out, and before the

security guard could stop me I had run over to the two men.

"What are you doing here, Diamond?" he snapped the moment he saw me.

Boyle curled his lip and looked ugly – which in his case wasn't very difficult. Once again he lumbered forward and grabbed hold of me.

"Don't worry, Boyle!" I said. "I haven't come here to steal your Barbie doll."

"Then why are you here?" Snape demanded.

"You've got to find Minerva," I began. "She's in danger."

"I know she's in danger," Snape replied. "Boyle and I are on special duty. We're looking after her."

"You don't understand…"

How could I tell them what I knew? There wasn't enough time and with all the noise in the place – the children screaming, the music playing, Rudolph singing and all the rest of it – I'd have been hoarse before I got to the end. But just then Minerva appeared, coming out of the grotto with her manager, Jake Hammill, next to her. There was no sign of her husband, but somehow I wasn't surprised.

I twisted out of Boyle's grip, and with Tim right behind me I ran over to her. As usual, Minerva was looking drop-dead gorgeous in a slinky, silver number, and despite everything I was glad that I had arrived in time and that she hadn't, after all, dropped dead. She was holding a present, about the size and shape of a shoe box. Santa must have just given it to her.

She saw me. "You!" she snapped – and unless that's Greek for Happy Christmas, she wasn't too pleased to see me.

I stood in front of her, my eyes fixed on the box. I didn't want to touch it. To be honest, I didn't want to be anywhere near it. I had a good idea what was inside.

"Did Santa give you that?" I demanded.

"Yes." She nodded.

"Do you know what it is?"

Minerva shrugged. She didn't really care. She was only here for the publicity. "No," she said.

"I think it's a clock," Tim chimed in.

"Why?"

"Well … I can hear it ticking."

Snape leant forward and took the box. "What's all this about?" he demanded.

"Chief Inspector," I said, and suddenly my mouth was dry. "I'd be very careful with that unless you want to spend this Christmas in six different parts of London all at the same time."

"What are you talking about?" Hammill demanded.

"There's probably an oak leaf or two in there and maybe some acorns. But I'll bet you any money that the rest of it is a bomb."

Maybe I said the word too loudly. Somehow the crowd caught on to what was happening and suddenly the entire department was filled with hysterical mothers dragging their screaming kids off to the nearest escalator. I ignored them. I just wanted to know if Snape was going to believe me. And to be fair to him, just this once he gave me the benefit of the doubt. Very gently, he lowered the box to the ground, then turned to Boyle. "Have you got a knife?" he asked.

Boyle reached into his pocket and took out first a cut-throat razor, then a bayonet and finally a flick knife. He pressed a button and ten centimetres of ugly steel leapt out to join in the cheerful Christmas atmosphere. Snape took it. Very carefully, he cut a square in the side of the parcel and peeled the cardboard back. He looked inside.

"He's right!" he said.

He didn't need to tell me. Looking over his shoulder, I could just make out part of an alarm clock, some loops of wire and something that could have been Plasticine but definitely wasn't.

Snape looked up. "Plastic explosive," he whispered. "It's connected to an alarm clock. It'll blow up when the bell goes." He squinted through the square he had cut out. Then, very slowly, he handed the package to Boyle. "All right, Boyle," he said. "This is timed to go off

315

in forty minutes. You'd better get it down to the bomb disposal squad."

"Where's that?" I asked.

"It's a forty-five-minute drive away."

Boyle stared at him.

"See if you can find a short cut," Snape advised.

Boyle disappeared – in a hurry. Snape turned to me. "So what's this all about?" he demanded.

"Santa just gave me that!" Minerva rasped. She was standing there dazed.

"Have you been a bad girl this year?" Tim asked.

"It's not Santa!" I said. "Come on…"

The five of us – me, Tim, Minerva, Jake Hammill and Snape – dived into the grotto. Out of the corner of my eye I saw the security guard talking into his radio, presumably calling for reinforcements. There was nobody else left on the fourth floor – as far as I knew, there was nobody left in Knightsbridge. White plastic snow crunched underfoot as we followed the path into the cave. White plastic stalactites hung down and white plastic stalagmites pointed up – or maybe it was the other way round. I can never remember. We passed a couple more mechanical singing reindeer and arrived just in time to see a familiar red figure, about to leave by a back exit.

"Hold it right there, Santa!" I shouted.

316

Santa froze, then slowly turned around.

"It's … it's … it's…!" Tim exclaimed. He stopped. He had no idea who it was, and with the red hood, the white beard and the golden-framed spectacles, I couldn't blame him. His own mother wouldn't recognize him. His own wife hadn't.

I walked forward and pulled off the beard. And there he was.

"Harold!" Minerva exclaimed.

"Harold?" Hammill quavered.

"That's right," I said. "Harold Chase."

There could be no doubt about it. The old man reached up and lowered the hood, revealing more of his face, his silver hair and his hearing aid. He had concealed his permanent suntan with make-up. But there could be no disguising the venom with which he was looking at his wife.

Snape took over. "You just gave Minerva a bomb," he said.

Harold Chase said nothing.

"That's a very original present," Tim commented.

"Not really, Tim," I said. "He was trying to kill her."

It was the word "kill" that did it. The bomb had been taken away. But Harold Chase exploded. "I hate her!" he screamed. "You have no idea what it's been like living with her! I know why she married me. She wanted my

317

money! But now that she's so big and so famous she doesn't need me. And so she humiliates and belittles me. She's made my life hell!"

He took a step towards us. Tim took three steps back.

"But that's not the worst of it," Harold went on. "She's a hypocrite. She smiles at the crowds on Regent Street when secretly she despises them. She hates Christmas too – and every year she's ruined it for me. No carols, no presents, no tinsel, no fun. She's stolen Christmas from me and that was a good enough reason to want to see her dead."

By now, he was frothing at the mouth and I almost wished Boyle was there to deal with him. Fortunately the security guard disguised as an elf had appeared with two colleagues, and the three of them dragged Harold out. He was still screaming as he went.

The five of us went back downstairs to a champagne bar on the ground floor. It was somewhere quiet and we had a lot to talk about. Minerva paid for champagne for herself and the others. I got a glass of lemonade. I had to admit she seemed very shaken by what had happened. Her face was pale. Her eyes were thoughtful. And even her silver-plated breasts seemed to have lost their sparkle.

"All right, Diamond," Snape said, emptying his glass. "Spit it out!"

"He hasn't drunk anything yet," Tim said.

"I want you to tell me what's been going on. How did you know about Harold Chase and how did you figure out his plan?"

"I worked it out when we visited Janey Winterbotham," I explained.

"The next-door neighbour?" Snape sniffed. "I spoke to her. She didn't tell me anything."

"She told me that Reginald Parker was an out-of-work actor but that he had a job in a department store every Christmas," I said. "What else could he have been but a department store Santa? That was when it all fell into place."

"Why don't you start at the beginning?" Jake Hammill suggested.

"All right." I drew a breath. "This is the way I see it. Harold Chase hated Minerva for all the reasons he just told us. His hatred had obviously driven him mad and he decided to kill her. But the trouble was, it was too obvious. If Minerva died, he would be the main suspect. Everyone knew how badly she treated him."

"A lot of people would die to be married to me," Minerva sniffed.

"He was married to you – and you were the one he wanted to die," I reminded her. "Anyway, Harold couldn't kill you himself. He'd be arrested at once. But then he had an idea. He realized that the best way to get rid of you was to create someone who didn't exist: a

319

crazy fan. He used that concert you cancelled – for Overweight Albanian Kids – and pretended that someone was out to get revenge."

"You mean … it was Harold who wrote that anonymous letter?" Hammill asked.

"Exactly. He even put a fake spelling mistake in it – but if he couldn't spell 'forgive', how come he could spell 'forget' a few lines later? The whole thing felt fake to me."

"And what about the cracker?"

"That was another clue. I thought at the time that there was something weird about it, but it was only later that I realized what it was." I turned to Hammill. "You'd booked Minerva into the Porchester hotel under a false name."

"Right," he said.

"But the box of crackers was addressed to her. Whoever sent it even knew the number of the suite where she was staying. It had to be an inside job."

"But wait a minute," Snape interrupted. "If it was Chase all the time, what was Reginald Parker doing on the roof at Regent Street?"

"Reginald Parker had been paid by Chase," I explained. "His neighbour told us he got a lot of money for a job in the West End. She probably thought it was a job in theatre. My guess is that Chase paid him to leave the silver oak leaves on the roof. Parker had no idea what he was doing. He didn't have a gun or anything. I saw him carrying something, but it could have been a camera. After all, he knew Minerva was there. He was a complete innocent. That's what he tried to tell me when I went up there. 'I didn't...' That was all he managed. But what he wanted to say was, 'I didn't do it!' He must have been horrified when he heard the shots."

"So who did shoot at me?" Minerva asked. She poured herself some more champagne. I wondered what she was celebrating. Maybe it was the fact she was still alive.

"That was Harold," I said. "Again, I'm only guessing, but I'd say he fired two blank shots from a gun he had inside his pocket. When we were on the platform, the shots sounded very close. He fired twice and then pointed to Reginald up on the roof – because, of course, he knew he'd be there. You see, he was creating the illusion of a killer ... someone who didn't really exist. The only snag is, the gun burnt a hole in his coat." I glanced at Minerva. "You thought he'd almost been hit. In fact, he'd fired the shots himself."

"I don't get it," Minerva exclaimed. "He wanted to protect me! It was Harold who persuaded me to get a bodyguard!"

"He did that to throw off any suspicion. At the same time, he made sure you hired the worst private detective in London. Someone too stupid to get in the way of his plan."

"And who was that?" Tim asked.

"Have some more champagne, Tim," I said.

"And then Harold Chase killed Reginald Parker," Snape said.

"You've got it in one, Chief Inspector. Chase had chosen Parker because he knew he was going to be the Santa Claus at Harrods. First of all he hired him to go on the roof. Then he killed him and took his place. Tim's business card must have fallen out of his pocket during the fight. It was when I saw the card that I put two and two together…"

"You did your maths homework?" Tim asked.

"No, Tim. I cracked the case."

There was a long silence. Either I'd been talking too slowly or they'd been drinking too quickly but all the champagne was gone. And I hadn't even touched my lemonade.

Jake Hammill put an arm around Minerva. "Baby, I'm so sorry," he said. "What a terrible experience for you!"

Minerva shrugged. "It wasn't so bad," she said. "I've got rid of Harold. I'm going to get lots of publicity. And my CD's certain to go to number one." She got to her feet. I thought she was going to leave, but she took one last look at me. "You're quite smart for a scruffy fourteen-year-old," she said. Then she flicked her eyes towards Tim. "As for you, you're just an utter loss."

She walked out.

"What did she mean?" Tim wailed.

I thought for a moment. "Justanutterloss. It's Greek for sensational," I said.

"Really?" Tim's eyes lit up.

"Sure, Tim," I said. Well, after all, it was Christmas.

There are a few things to add.

Two weeks later, Tim and I got a surprise in the post – and this time it wasn't a bomb, an unpaid bill or a poison pen letter. It was a note from Jake Hammill. It seemed that he wasn't so bad after all. We had just saved his most famous client from a murder attempt that would have been not only the end of her career, but – even worse – the end of his percentage. And as a token of his gratitude, he'd decided to send us a cheque for ten thousand pounds. I'll never forget the sight of Tim holding it between his hands. The last time he had seen that many zeros, it had been in his school report.

We talked a lot about what to do with the money. Of course, we were going to have a proper Christmas lunch. Tim was going to pay off the rent. I was finally going to get a new school uniform – the last one had so many patches in it, it was more patches than uniform. But that would still leave us with several thousand pounds, which was just about the most money we'd ever had.

I forget who suggested it first, but that was when we decided to fly out to Australia to be reunited with our parents. It had been years since we'd seen them, and sometimes I thought it was unnatural for a young lad to be living without his mother, often crying himself to sleep, having to be tucked in every night and cheered up by his brother. Not that I minded doing all that for Tim, but even so I thought it would do us all good to be a family again, just for a while.

And the next day we bought two British Airways tickets to Sydney. We were going to travel out as soon as the Easter term ended, and maybe one day I'll write down what actually happened when we got there. *The Radius of the Lost Shark*. That's the title I've got written down in my notebook. It's another story I've got to tell.

What else is there? Harold Chase got life in jail for attempted murder, but looking at him I didn't think that would be too many years. Snape took the credit for the arrest, of course. They actually put his face on the front cover of the monthly police journal, *Hello, Hello, Hello* magazine. Reginald Parker's remains were scattered in the River Thames, in front of the National Theatre – as he'd requested in his will. It can't have been pleasant, though. He hadn't been cremated.

And what about Minerva? She may have got to number one, but I didn't care. I never listened to her music again. She may have had everything, but without a heart you're just nothing. She was like a December without Christmas – and at the end of the day, what's the point of that?

MORE BOOKS
BY ANTHONY
HOROWITZ...

THE ALEX RIDER SERIES

Alex Rider – you're never too young to die…

High in the Alps, death waits for Alex Rider…

Sharks. Assassins. Nuclear bombs. Alex Rider's in deep water.

Alex Rider has 90 minutes to save the world.

Once stung, twice as deadly. Alex Rider wants revenge.

He's back – and this time there are no limits.

ANTHONY HOROWITZ

THE POWER OF FIVE

FIVE ORDINARY TEENAGERS.
FIVE EXTRAORDINARY POWERS.

ONE CHANCE
TO SAVE
MANKIND.

OBLIVION

THE FINAL THRILLING EPISODE
UNLEASHED AUTUMN 2012.

FIND OUT HOW IT ALL BEGAN...
WWW.POWEROF5.CO.UK

THE POWER OF FIVE

RAVEN'S GATE

DARKNESS WAITS ON
THE OTHER SIDE...

He always knew he was
different. First there were the
dreams. Then the deaths began.

ANTHONY
HOROWITZ

THE POWER OF FIVE

EVIL
STAR

WHEN IT FLICKERS
THE WORLD DIES...

It began with Raven's Gate.
But it's not over yet.
Once again the enemy is stirring.

ANTHONY
HOROWITZ

NIGHT
RISE

WHO WILL LIVE TO
SEE ANOTHER DAY?

Darkness covers the earth.
The Old Ones have returned.
The battle must begin.

ANTHONY
HOROWITZ

NECROPOLIS

WELCOME TO THE
CITY OF THE DEAD

An ancient evil is unleashed.
Five have the power to defeat it.
But one of them has been taken.

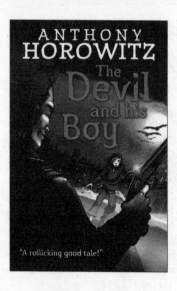

London is dirty, distant and dangerous ... but that's where orphan Tom Falconer is heading. And he's got a whole assortment of vicious criminals hot on his heels.

Tom is helpless and alone until he meets Moll Cutpurse, a thirteen-year-old pickpocket. Together the two of them find themselves chased across the city by the murderous Ratsey. But it's only on the first night of a new play – *The Devil and his Boy* – that Tom realizes the fate of the Queen and indeed the entire country rests in his hands.

All the pace, excitement and last minute escapes readers expect from an Anthony Horowitz novel are here, in a vivid and realistic Elizabethan setting.

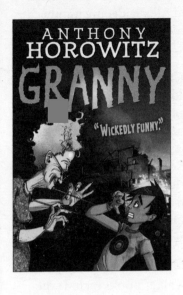

He could see it in the wicked glimmer in her eyes, in the half-turned corner of her mouth. And it was so strong, so horrible that he shivered. She was evil.

"Wickedly funny."
Daily Telegraph

"A hoot... Anthony Horowitz has created a scary and unmissable old hag."
Daily Mail

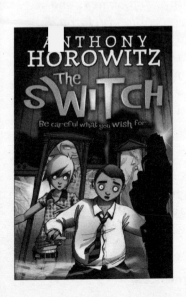

Be careful what you wish for...

Tad Spencer has everything a boy could want – incredibly rich parents, and a whole summer ahead to enjoy however he pleases. Until one evening he makes the huge mistake of wishing he was someone else.

ANTHONY HOROWITZ is one of the most popular contemporary children's writers. Both The Power of Five and Alex Rider are number one bestselling series enjoyed by millions of readers worldwide.

When Anthony launched the Alex Rider series he created a phenomenon in children's books, spurring a new trend of junior spy books and inspiring thousands of previously reluctant readers. Hailed as a reading hero, Anthony has also won many major awards, including the Bookseller Association/Nielsen Author of the Year Award, the Children's Book of the Year Award at the British Book Awards, and the Red House Children's Book Award. The first Alex Rider adventure, *Stormbreaker*, was made into a blockbuster movie in 2006.

Anthony's other titles for Walker Books include the Diamond Brothers mysteries; *Groosham Grange* and its sequel, *Return to Groosham Grange*; *The Devil and His Boy*; *Granny*; *The Switch*; and a collection of horror stories, *More Bloody Horowitz*. Anthony also writes extensively for TV, with programmes including *Foyle's War*, *Midsomer Murders*, *Collision* and, most recently, *Injustice*. His latest novel, *The House of Silk*, is a brand new Sherlock Holmes adventure, written with the endorsement of the Conan Doyle Estate.

Although abandoned by both his sons, Anthony Horowitz continues to live in Clerkenwell with his wife, Jill Green, and the ghost of his dog, Lucky. You can find out more about Anthony and his books at:

www.anthonyhorowitz.com

www.alexrider.com

www.powerof5.co.uk